William Rivière

William Rivière was born in 1954 and brought up in Norfolk. After leaving King's College, Cambridge, he spent several years in Venice. Later he worked in Japan and travelled around the Far East, paddling sampans in Sarawak and sailing lateen craft in the Indian Ocean. WATERCOLOUR SKY, his first novel, won a Betty Trask Award on its publication in 1990. It has been followed by A VENETIAN THEORY OF HEAVEN, EROS AND PSYCHE, BORNEO FIRE and, most recently, ECHOES OF WAR. He has one son and is married to a painter, and has returned to Italy where he teaches at the University of Urbino.

SCEPTRE

Also by William Rivière

A Venetian Theory of Heaven
Eros and Psyche
Borneo Fire
Echoes of War

Watercolour Sky

WILLIAM RIVIÈRE

SCEPTRE

First published in the UK in 1990 by Hodder and Stoughton
A division of Hodder Headline PLC
A Sceptre Paperback

10 9 8 7 6 5 4 3 2

British Library Cataloguing in Publication Data

Rivière, William
  Watercolour sky.
  I. Title
  823'.914 [F]

  ISBN 0 340 54571 2

Typeset by Palimpsest Book Production Limited,
Polmont, Stirlingshire
Printed and bound in Great Britain by
Caledonian International Book Manufacturers, Glasgow

Hodder and Stoughton
A division of Hodder Headline PLC
338 Euston Road
London NW1 3BH

"The words of Mercury are harsh after the songs of Apollo. You, that way: we, this way."

Love's Labour's Lost

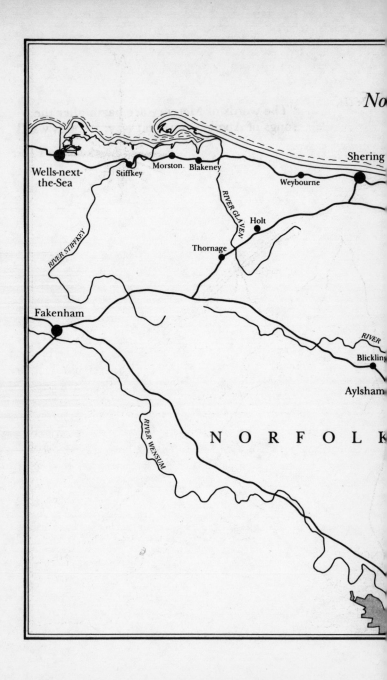

No

Shering

Wells-next-
the-Sea

Stiffkey

Morston

Blakeney

Weybourne

RIVER GLAVEN

Holt

RIVER STIFFKEY

Thornage

Fakenham

RIVER

Blicklin

Aylsham

N O R F O L K

RIVER WENSUM

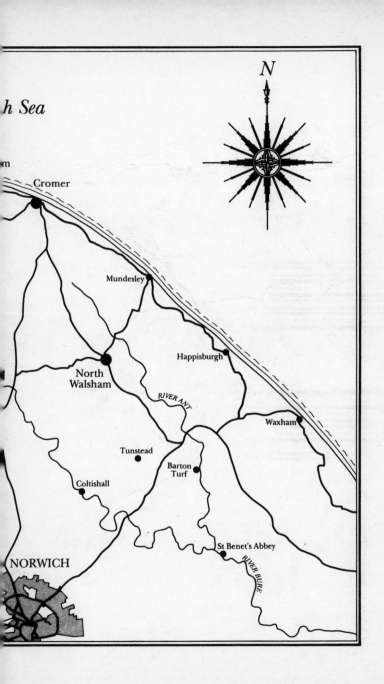

h Sea

Cromer

Mundesley

North
Walsham

Happisburgh

RIVER ANT

Waxham

Tunstead

Barton
Turf

Coltishall

St Benet's Abbey

RIVER BURE

NORWICH

N

ONE

I

Sails.

Sails far away across salt marsh, far away in Blakeney creek in evening light waiting for the start.

White, white, blue, red or tan, white. Which of the white sails was *Trio*'s? *Scandal*'s sails were blue. Who had reddish sails, brownish? Not *Avocet*, not *Fiducia*, not *Sea Pink*. Was it *Snark* or *Vanity*?

"Which is *Trio*? Oh, Mummy, which is *Trio*?"

"I can't tell, Alice. They're a mile off. More."

"When will they start?"

"Watch. The slowest boats will start any minute now."

"I wish you'd let me crew Daddy."

Thérèse was crewing him. Thérèse was standing on wet mud and sea lavender holding *Trio*'s forestay, waiting for the handicapper to check his stopwatch and grin and call, "*Trio* away!" Then Daddy would call, "Push off!" and Thérèse would push and jump.

Emma Dobell stood in the attic of Morston Manor, her dead parents' house, and smiled at her daughter hunched on the sill. Out in the harbour mouth, the tide had been setting for three or four hours, sluicing in brown and grey over the mussel beds, lifting grounded buoys on their slimy warps. Soon there would be enough water in the Pit for the race to start. In the deep water, the anchored fishing-smacks,

11

that had lain to the north wind, had swung round to the west to face the tide.

"He has Mr Clabburn to crew him and he has Thérèse. She's thirteen, darling, you're seven." Emma sat down on the child's truckle bed, set the cold slippery cocktail shaker on the floorboards, took a swig of her martini, lit a cigarette. "Perhaps next Morston regatta, next year . . ."

"I can crew. I can pull in the jib sheet when the wind's not too strong." Alice stopped, then added honestly, "I can't pull up the plate."

Emma laughed. "I can only just pull it up. And only Benedict can hoist the gaff."

She lifted a dark strand of hair across her eyes, looked through it at her younger child's blonde head, cigarette smoke hazing the open window, the coast and fields where she had grown up. From the west, the sun flung warm swathes of golden light along the shore, swathes that shifted so slowly they appeared still. From the north, the wind harried white tatters high and fast and cold across the blue; down where people could feel it, the buffeting sea wind scudded ashore, leaped slightly to clear the dunes, shingle banks, mud-flats, rushed on south up the gentle incline into the low-lying land. The attic window rattled.

I'm his daughter, Alice thought, Thérèse isn't his daughter, I am. But it made her face hot to think that, so she leaned out into the soughing air with her back to her mother who mustn't know her bad thoughts and mustn't think sad thoughts about Thérèse's father who was dead in . . . Oh, where, dead where? – not France – but somewhere like France – oh, why didn't she remember things? And why did it make her face burn more? And why couldn't she turn round and ask?

"Your father loves it when you sail with him. But not in a race, not in an evening race."

"What's the time? I don't have to get into bed yet."

"Watch or you'll miss the start."

"Will they fire a starting gun?"

"Yes, but we won't hear it."

Alice's heart cried, Sails why won't you come? White,

blue, tan sails, why won't you stop slatting and come one by one, in twos and threes, out of the creek into the bay heading for the first buoy?

Emma sang,

It was a lover and his lass . . .

More and more when she had nothing to say and didn't want to think she sang. Not only at such times. But often. And everyone liked it when she sang. The trouble with this song was that Alice knew the refrain. In she chimed now with her clear child's voice, she liked this bit,

With a hey, and a ho, and a hey nonino . . .

But a little girl's singing that was practically shouting wasn't the trouble. The trouble was twenty years of gin and cigarettes. The trouble was a war some knew how to outlive and some didn't. Then further wars and one husband dead and the other too good for her, too innocent.

Between the acres of the rye . . .

No rye in Norfolk and no oats to speak of. Just one hell of a lot of wheat and barley and sugarbeet. And fresh marsh and salt marsh. This coast of low muddy cliffs and longshore-drift, beaches and estuaries. A flint church every mile or two. You ride a horse along the shore from graveyard to graveyard, sail offshore from tower to tower. Samphire, windmills, migratory birds, wide North Sea skies – what was the reason these things now gave her such faint pleasure? They meant the years of *l'entre deux guerres*, the thirties when her whole world was going to hell but she as it chanced had been happy enough, just any child growing up on a peaceful coast. Then in sea-light the countless ply of the mind, that in Emma's head were normally jammed warping together, lay evenly and lightly – or so she recalled, wondering why it rarely felt like that now. Still, luckily you could infuse into your children those delights you no longer felt; they wouldn't realise how forced it was, if they ever realised, till long afterward.

Alice's face had gone from too hot to too cold. She shivered, cuddled her dressing-gown round her lest she be ordered to shut the window. She heard the chink and slosh as her mother tipped the shaker over her glass. Down below lay the orchard in its walls of flint. But it was too near the sea, Daddy said, the salt wind meant the apples and pears were never as good as in the orchard at Fen House ten miles inland. Across the lane stood the gale-beaten and brick-patched church on its knoll where they trooped up on Sundays and Daddy stood at the lectern in his tweed suit to read the lesson. Once after church she found a rabbit crawling on a grave. Why won't it run away? she asked, and what's wrong with its eyes? Leave it, her father told her, it's got myxomatosis. It's dying, there's nothing you can do.

"Will *Trio* win?"

"Benedict has come second, third, second. One year he may win."

"Why is it called the Battle of Morston Creek?"

"There have been some rare battles."

"Pirates?" Alice dreamed.

"Not exactly piracy. But boats gone aground, masts broken. It can be quite a fight beating up Morston creek to the finishing line against an ebb tide."

"*Trio* will win when you and I crew Daddy," Alice said with her wind-cold face turned to her mother, her eyes fierce with her half-forgotten shame and her love.

"One day you may win the Battle."

"I want to win the Muck Boats' Cup. I want Daddy to win it now and me later."

Muck Boats. That was what they were. Just old Muck Boats, local craft, no two alike, clinker-built and gunter-rigged. Alice knew all about Muck Boats. That was easier than where people died, men you could never know, countries you might never see. Mr Balding built *Trio* before the war, and some of the other vessels too. He kept his cows on their meadow. Alice craned her neck toward the sea. Yes, there were the Ayrshires, then the thorns, the marsh. That was where the new sea-wall would be built, Daddy said. It would keep the marsh tides at bay. A few winters before she was born, on a night with an onshore gale the sea crossed the marsh and raged into the villages, it rose chest-deep in the manor kitchen, you could still see the tide-line left on the wall by the salt. Secretly, Alice longed for that to happen again before the sea-wall was built, before she grew and the tide-line was only waist-high.

Mr Clabburn and her father and Mr Balding and somebody else kept their sails, gaffs and booms in the falling-down sail-shed by the hard. The boats lay at their moorings along Morston creek. *Trio* had a bowsprit. Mr Balding never took his sails and spars down from the rafters any more, he was too old to sail, soon he would die. In the winter *Trio* came on a farm trailer with a tractor to pull it and then she lay in the manor barn.

"Thérèse will be nervous," Emma said. "Those sails battering. When they start and the sails are sheeted in and quiet it's better."

"I wonder if she's fallen in the creek."

"Don't be silly. Mr Clabburn will help her hold *Trio*. That boat pulls like a frightened horse."

Tonight *Trio* would be back on her mooring. That was a good thing to know, Alice set herself to think it. No longer away beyond the pilot path, beyond those flat bluish greenish miles, away in Blakeney creek under Blakeney church. And not thrashing about the harbour either, not rounding buoys in Blakeney Pit. No. Back on her mooring in Morston creek, whether vanquisher of the other Muck Boats or not. Back lying between *Sea Pink* and *Vanity*, who were rivals for one tide a year but companionable spirits for all the rest. Her bilges would be bailed dry with a tin scoop (that would be Thérèse's job) and her sails would be carried back to the shed as twilight came and the tide went down.

"Can I come downstairs when Daddy and Thérèse get back?"

"Yes, of course you can. I should think Dick Clabburn will come in for a glass of whisky. Oh look, they're off!"

"I didn't hear the gun!"

"Too far."

Oh come, Alice prayed, oh come, sails, come, sails.

II

Jolt and splash. Then black ooze rising unstoppably quickly up black boot. Then ooze lapping over the rim and flowing down inside. Alice Dobell swayed, grabbed a slippery whippy willow branch. Wet corduroy leg, wet sock, smell of ditch, cold foot.

She heaved. Her foot came easily, her boot glugged and stayed. She let go of the willow, snatched for her boot, pitched her weight to fall sideways onto the sedge which frost had laid every-which-way brown and lifeless on the sodden earth.

Woodcock! Benedict Dobell stood still to let the brown bird fly off through the alders. He preferred not to shoot woodcock and not to shoot hares . . . and Dr Mack, whose woods here at Abbot's Hall he was walking now with the children, let him do as he pleased. Dobell mildly wished some of his other neighbours would let the woodcock and hares restore their numbers in peace. But you couldn't urge men to do this or that on their land. You could only try to spread ideas without anyone noticing . . .

Snipe too. There were nothing like the snipe he remembered as a boy before the war. But not many people shot well enough to kill a lot of snipe – the way they jigged and jinked up from the fresh marshes. It was farmers draining marshland, it was fertilisers and pesticides – and they finished off a lot of wild flowers and butterflies too.

Thérèse now, she was getting to be a fine shot . . . The first day of every Christmas holiday he took her to shoot clay pigeons. Each time he rejoiced in the instructor's surprise and admiration. Whether the girl rejoiced it was hard to tell, her glasses were so protective, her manner was so still.

He glanced sidelong. Amidst the leafless oaks, willows, the odd Scots fir, his stepdaughter stood still and raised one hand. She looked as thin and frail as the reeds. Her green coat was darkened by rain, she was the lichen colour of the dripping trees. Her short black hair flattened by rain glistened, her glasses glistened, her gun glistened on her arm.

Dobell raised his hand to show he understood. Their solitary beater on this most modest but finest of days shooting was down in the mire again. Her blonde head was the only bright thing in the wood.

Alice saw her father's cavalry-twill legs and tweed shoulders pushing through the reeds. The wet earth seeped through to her hip and elbow. Her capsized rubber boot lay hull-down in slime among foundered branches, a modern wreck gone down to join wooden ships that sank long ago.

"My stick! I've lost my holly stick!"

"Let's rescue you and your boot first."

She saw him take the cartridges out of his twelve-bore and lean it against a tree, hoik her boot out of the ditch. When he took off his tweed cap, she saw the faint rim it left on his fair cropped head. When he bent over her, hauled her up, shoved her leg into her boot, she smelled his cheroots and his eau de Cologne.

"There's my stick."

The holly her father had whittled for her gleamed where it lay on the mud. He picked it up, recalling how young Thérèse had been when she had extricated herself from the ditches she fell into. Well, people grew up in fits and starts.

Dobell recollected the first pheasant he had shot. His uncle had the shooting over at Thornage in the thirties. The beaters went into an old marl pit overgrown with sycamore and thorn. The guns stood on ploughland: cousins, neighbours, friends, Benedict's older brother whose first pheasant had been shot there two winters before, borne home in triumph to Fen House.

Ten-year-old Benedict's frozen feet and hands and face ached, his eyes watered in the blizzard that swept the arable wastes. All the shots he had missed made his chest feel hollow and at the same time heavy, made his head feel hollow and light. Then a cock pheasant got up, wretchedly he saw it was coming over him, he heard his father say Yours Benedict, he would have to try and to fail yet again, he cocked the right barrel of the hammer .410. Old Wellington the keeper stopped by the spinney to watch. It was an easy shot, Benedict saw to his dismay, there would be no more excuse than ever, he fired. Then he was standing with the left hammer untouched, forgotten utterly, watching the cock dip in his flight. He was winged, was he? Perhaps, not badly. He lost height gradually, cleared a fence . . .

Benedict Dobell did not understand why the most intense of his selves had for thirty years been standing quivering on a ploughed field with a lowered shot-gun in his childish hands while a pheasant, recently quivering, more recently knocked on the head behind a hedge, was brought to him by a gamekeeper. But it was so. That Asiatic plumage carried in Anglo-Saxon hands, that wintry covert, that elegant Victorian weapon with its chasing and its sheen, had all the romance of disappointment, the most enrapturing romance of all.

To thank old Wellington with your voice for having his dog retrieve your bird; to thank him with your eyes – voluntarily? involuntarily? – for having finished the messy job you'd made of it . . . was that the conduct one had to learn? No – better not thank him with your eyes. But to kill your own provender sometimes, to resolve to learn to kill cleanly . . . To do things not particularly good but better done than undone, to take the tawdry evidence of your existence from Wellington's hands because that was more honourable and more humorous than to say that a soul lived in your breast – was that the style to rehearse? Was

19

that *la gaia scienza*, to take the insignificant corpse and say thank you and walk back to the farm cart?

A generation later, the line of three human beings and a dog reformed. Alice Dobell thwacked the thickets stolidly with her holly stick, she tore and stumbled through dead bramble, dead rush. She heard the clatter of wings, the light crack of the .410, turned, saw a hen pheasant fly away, saw Thérèse bend her head to take out a spent cartridge and put in another. It was the old double-barrelled .410, why didn't Thérèse shoot twice? Out of range? Alice was hazy about range.

But next year she would inherit the .410, that winter would be magical. Daddy was going to buy Thérèse a twenty-eight-bore. Would it be nice for Thérèse to have a new gun that ejected spent cartridges automatically so she didn't have to pluck them out with cold fingers and those nails she bit? The twelve-bore was old, it had been Benedict's father's gun; but it jerked out cartridges with an oily gun-metallic click; Alice liked watching them leap backward and fall; sometimes she picked up the brass caps and red cardboard tubes to breathe the gunpowder. Or would Thérèse regret the .410 with its hammers you had to cock with your cold slithery thumb, its double barrels longer and more stylish than those of a modern .410? And would Alice ever learn to cock it quickly enough to shoot any bird while it was still in range?

They had walked two woods, a field of kale, hedgerows, a marsh. Alice's legs ached. The downpour had drenched her collar, seeped inside her coat, now it was working down her jersey and shirt. She wanted to call Dusk to talk to him; but her father held strong views on the training of gun-dogs, he kept Dusk near him, quartering the ground close to his master's left and right, never bounding far ahead, never lagging behind wasting time on seductive but unprofitable scents.

When he came out of the wood, Benedict Dobell had three pheasants in his game-bag. And lucky he was to have them, he reflected. It was twenty years since Abbot's Hall had been run as a shoot; there was no keeper, no game was

20

reared. And when you did get a shot you were more often than not knee-deep in bog; or you couldn't see the bird that got up because the wood was so tangled; or the single pheasant in a fen would get up when you had unloaded to scramble over a dyke.

Dr Mack rarely got his gun to his shoulder in time to shoot anything these days. Benedict Dobell and Dick Clabburn were the only neighbours he ever invited to come and walk round, and that was only because their fathers had shot here. There was Dick now, standing on the meadow in smearing drizzle, whistling to his spaniel. The dog came trotting through the thistles and cow pats with a pheasant in its mouth.

Dobell walked across to young Robert Clabburn.

"Is that your bird?"

"Yes," the boy said, trying not to sound pleased, his breaking voice jumping from growl to squeak. "It was a runner I'm afraid, but Hedge caught it. Perhaps I ought to . . ."

He looked nervously to where his father was taking the fluttering body from the spaniel.

"Perhaps you should," Dobell said gently. "But well done shooting it."

He watched the boy walk away to his father. Would Dick make his son wring the bird's neck? No, he was doing it himself.

Dr Mack had shot nothing. He stood on the bleak grass like the stump of a storm-ruined oak, short, bowed, motionless. Rain slithered down his ancient brown sou'wester and torn brown mackintosh. One gnarled hand in its torn shooting mitten was crabbed onto his blackthorn, the other hung limp under the chasing on his gun.

"Boy shot well," he said. "Your girl get a shot?"

"She missed a hen bird."

Alice was patting Dusk, yellow-headed child bent over yellow labrador. Thérèse stood alone at the wood side.

"There may be mallard on the river. Let her walk up."

"Right."

"Then you and Clabburn walk the home wood. You never know," the old man's eyes laughed, "they rear a lot of game across the river, some of them may have come over my side. I'll stand on the back drive. Bring the wood toward me. Then we'll walk the garden. Then lunch."

The pattern of a morning's rough shooting at Abbot's Hall never changed. Dobell liked that. Sometimes he was given instructions; sometimes they were omitted. He always did the same things in the same order; they were always the right things to do. Even the jokes about Blickling pheasants coming over the water were reliable – old jokes were just as funny, perhaps funnier, than new.

Their host watched Dobell go across to his stepdaughter. Odd girl, she didn't move or speak. Odd having a girl shooting anyhow, the old man mused. But Dobell had no son, so . . . He watched him point out to the child which way to approach the river so as not to be seen till the last moment. She took off her spectacles, wiped them, put them on again. Bad luck she needed spectacles. Hadn't her father been a pilot? He must have had good eyesight . . .

———◆———

Dr Mack crept away among the stag-headed oaks toward his house, blackthorn pegging along shakily, ill-trained black retriever lolloping ahead. Dobell and Clabburn strode the longer way round the water-meadow to enter the home wood from the far side. Robert hastened after the men, his mind glorious with how he would tell his mother he had shot his fifth or was it his sixth pheasant. The dogs trotted after their masters, Alice stumbled along behind Dusk. Rain drilled down more heavily.

Away on her own, going the longest way round, Thérèse was walking as quietly as she could toward the river. Peewits mewed and tumbled overhead. Benedict, watching her ceaselessly, saw her stop, find a dryish patch of shirt-tail, mop her glasses again, forget to tuck her shirt in. On she went, head bowed as she came to the river bank.

The duck might be upstream, downstream, had he dispatched her to the right place? The rond along the river hardly rose from the flat field, the reedbeds were reduced by winter, even a child bent nearly double couldn't get very close without being sensed. The rain was lucky. But still . . . And the hammers on that old .410 were difficult to cock.

Wildfowl whirled up from the river into the grey rinsing air. Her stepfather saw Thérèse fling up her gun, crack, a mallard dropped out of the scattering skein, she swung further, crack, a second shadow was faltering sideways and down, hard hit but not dead, by God she's done it, a right and left, Thérèse *victrix*, by God I love that girl.

Dick Clabburn muttered, "Damned good," an astonished grin on his pink rainy face.

Dobell nodded silently. Not Thérèse de Nérac, Thérèse *victrix*, strange, why had he thought that?

"Hedge!" shouted Robert with a cracking voice, calling in his father's dog unnecessarily, the dead pheasant hanging from his hand suddenly horrible, pitiful.

Alice ran. Tussocks tripped her, her boots squelched. She wanted to throw away her stick but then remembered, it was her holly stick, her white peeled stick.

"Well shot, Thérèse!" Thérèse said nothing. "Where are they? A left and right!" Or did one say right and left? Right. Left. Hayfoot, strawfoot. "Where . . . ?"

Thérèse trudged along the rond between the meadow and the grey sliding stream, her half-sister burbling at her heels. She pointed to a small dark floating lump. That was the first, swirling away. She swung her pointing arm to the second, the wounded bird, being picked by Dusk as they watched.

"Mark my mallard in the river, Alice," she said suddenly.

"Mark it . . . ?" Alice wondered.

"Yes," she said. "Run downstream. Never take your eyes off it."

Alice watched Thérèse swing away from the river, tramp quickly toward Benedict. What was she . . . ? The duck!

Alice jerked her eyes back to the eddying passing water. Help! Was that it? She blushed scarlet alone in the rain. No, that was a clod of – or a tuft of – or no was it . . . ? Oh help! Why did she always . . . ?

Benedict Dobell didn't move. Simultaneously Thérèse and Dusk reached him from opposite sides. The girl's mouth showed nothing, and behind her glasses, behind the waterdrops beading and trickling on each lens, how could one tell if she were pleased? Certainly the child could never be accused of showing off. But some pleasure in achievement she must feel? Is she *just* shooting for the pot? Doing what's expected, what comes?

"A right and left of mallard with a .410," he said temperately, "is fine shooting, at thirteen or at any age."

He said it to the black soaked hair on her nape, because she was stooped over Dusk who was trained to retrieve only to his master but made an exception of Thérèse. She handed her unloaded gun to Dobell, took the wounded drake, held its body between her two hands, glanced round for something hard against which to knock its head. There was nothing. The man watched the girl realise, saw her mouth wince. I'll do it, he could say. But already she had forced her left hand to shift from the bird's body to its throat, let go with her right, swung the body but swung it too feebly, tightened the grip of her thin blood-stained fingers, swung viciously, wrung the duck's neck.

"Well shot, Thérèse," Robert said, pronouncing her name with his schoolboy accent. "Is it your first right and left?"

"Yes."

"I've never shot a right and left."

"Your pheasant just now was a good shot."

"How could you see? You were in the wood."

"They told me," Thérèse said, who had spoken with nobody.

Alice cast to and fro along the rond frenzied by her own distractedness. Was that a drifting duck? Oh what would Thérèse say? Nothing probably. That would be the worst thing about it. Had the bird sunk? That was a clump of

24

weed. Did dead bodies float or sink? She consulted her store of literary knowledge, the stories Benedict and Emma had read aloud. There must be something in *The Swiss Family Robinson* on the subject – but what? If she were dropped dead from the sky into a swollen December river what would . . . ? In *The Wind in the Willows* was there a . . . ? She slipped on mud pocked and slimed where cattle had come to drink, fell with her hand in dung.

"Go fetch! Good Hedge, good girl." A hundred yards downstream Clabburn, who knew how fast even sluggish Norfolk rivers will carry a shot bird away, who had walked straight to where he knew the child's mallard would be, hullooed his dog into the water. "Go fetch, go on, get in there!"

Alice and Dusk, sent through the thick in the home wood, had their world canopied by huge rhododendrons, their zigzag ways barred by fallen rotting trees. She put up a pheasant that she never saw, heard her father call "Forward!" but heard no shot; Dr Mack must have taken too long discarding his blackthorn, disentangling the leash on his whimpering fretting dog.

The sapless undergrowth smelled of freshwater and loam. Here a decrepit oak had been converted to an ivy tod; the brown lacing and the green dripping leaves must be full of decaying nests; she stopped to peer in but found none. There an ash tree when it fell had lifted a ten foot hood of mossy earth making a cave festooned with roots with a black puddle for floor. Dusk backed out, it didn't smell of rabbit; his wet muddy hindquarters and tail transferred more soil onto his adorer's face as she followed on hands and knees. Once in the cave she stayed, being dripped on by the black earth roof, wrapped in her hiddenness, dreaming vaguely. Oars were made of ash, her father had told her, they used to call them the white ash breeze.

For a generation there had been no horses in the stables. Under a catalpa tree, a dog cart rotted, shafts sticking up into the boughs. In the garden, the flower beds had lain fallow so long it was hard to tell where they had been. Alice beat her way tiredly through barricades of leggy lilac and azalea toward the silent ivied house, half its windows always shuttered, broken gutters spilling rain.

She came to the boggy hollow that had been a lily pond when Maria Pasqua Mack walked there on paved paths long disappeared. Alice loved to imagine her clothes – were they mouldering in wardrobes upstairs? Ladies wore such dresses in her great-great-aunt's scrapbook; on winter evenings she spread it on the library hearthrug, pored over those frills and furbelows. Maria Pasqua came from Naples, Daddy said; she was dancing in a theatre in Paris and Dr Mack's father fell in love with her and married her and brought her home to Abbot's Hall.

There was Robert Clabburn standing on the far side of the dell.

"Hullo, Alice. Your face is covered with mud."

"So is yours." Robert was her father's godson, Dusk liked Robert, Alice liked Robert. He was the only boy in the world with roan hair. His face had nothing like as much mud on it as hers, but he would understand she was just being friendly. "There are no pheasants here."

"I'm hungry."

"Me too."

"What's that shed?"

"Chapel."

"*Chapel?*"

"Dr Mack is a Roman Catholic," Alice explained. Didn't Mr Clabburn tell Robert anything? "He's half Italian."

The chapel didn't look much bigger than a loose-box, the window was broken, a faint way lay through brambles to the paintless door. Did Dr Mack sometimes go in to pray? Did a priest ever come?

They wound through a stand of yews to the ruined conservatory. Robert unloaded his twenty-bore and in they went. Broken glass, broken shelves. Sills and beams rotted with winters' rains. Rusted watering-cans, rusted trowels, rusted stove and boiler and pipes. Smashed terracotta, dead plants, dead birds.

"Dr Mack," pronounced Alice, "once discovered an orchid."

"Oh yes?" asked Robert, who was in his first year at Harrow and believed in being polite to young girls. "Where?"

"South America." She faltered. "I think."

"What did he call it? What does it look like?"

Orinoco, Amazon . . . Plate? Different question, wrong answer.

"Now it's at Kew."

————— ◆◆◆◆ —————

The three dogs' feet on the hall floor skittered, their wagging tails made a flumping sound against everybody's trouser legs, so did game-bags chucked down on the window seat. Guns were laid gently on the table with a light knock. Mr Clabburn's cartridge-belt went down on the sideboard with a snaky double fall. Alice picked it up, saw the form in the dust where it had lain, let it fall again and listened.

She liked Abbot's Hall being so dusty. Dr Mack had a woman come to clean once a week, but she was only let sweep the floor, nothing above ankle level was ever disturbed. Alice would have liked to live in a house so jumbled with grimy half-incomprehensible things, in rooms so still and quiet with the stillness and quietness of decades of the untouched, the unchanged, the unsaid. When she tried to explain this to her mother, Emma Dobell said she preferred to sit in armchairs not dim and rank with the hairs of retrievers long buried, preferred to drink from a washed glass, approved of roses that grew on the outside walls of drawing-rooms not the inside, approved of library shelves dry enough to stop the books growing mould. Fussy, her younger daughter thought.

The good ship *Peggy* was wrecked off Mundesley. Here was a vast wooden lantern from her poop, hanging now from a beam in the hall. Over the fireplace hung fowling-pieces, their barrels ever more pitted with rust, though over the years both Dobell and Clabburn had suggested, tactfully and without success, that they lift them down and oil them. Viced in a wooden press on the sideboard lay a second edition of Dr Johnson's dictionary, now with a cartridge-bag on it, dictionary and sideboard and press gnawed equally by the same worms.

Marvellous house in which you could wander into any room wearing muddy boots and no one cared. Alice followed Dr Mack's bowed back to the scullery. She washed her hands with coal tar soap under the cold tap, watched Thérèse and Robert lay out four brace of pheasant, a brace of mallard, a rabbit and a woodpigeon on the flagged floor.

In the kitchen they sat on Windsor chairs with splinted limbs and with amputations, on frowsty armchairs with wrung withers and hamstrung legs, chairs disfigured as with repeated child-bearing. Up by the cornice bulged the rusty bells whose jangling had summoned Maria Pasqua's maids, though now her son holed up in the kitchen because the aga made it the only warm room in the house. From the bells, mummified by cobwebs, dangled wires on which speck of dust had accrued to speck of dust for so long that they were soft and furry as caterpillars, and twice the width they had been when they twitched with the currents of life.

Smell of wet jerseys and wet dogs. Benedict opened the old biscuit tins in which his wife had packed pheasant sandwiches, bacon sandwiches, Bath Olivers, Stilton, Cheddar, hardboiled eggs, Egremont Russets from the orchard at Fen House. He poured soup from a thermos for Dr Mack, poured soup for the children. He should have insisted Alice take off her wet boots, she looked wan with weariness, gazing through the scummed window at rain on rough grass that had been a lawn, absently patting Dusk with hands that were washed but not clean.

Hunched in his leather waistcoat, in his ravelling cardigan over it, in his ravelling Norwich shawl over that, scarf still round his withered sallow throat, filthy shooting mittens still on his yellow hands, Dr Mack mumblingly ate one of Emma's sandwiches.

"Where was this shot?" he demanded, meaning the cold pheasant in his mouth.

"Hoveton."

"I haven't shot there for ten years." He frowned at the thermos, the wicker baskets, the tins and cups on his kitchen table. "There's a case of stout in the pantry. Who knows where it is?"

Dick Clabburn stood up, laid his sandwich tin on his chair, went out. Dr Mack's black labrador bitch bent her head over the tin. Robert was the first to notice. Concern for his father's lunch and health fought and won an instant's battle with reluctance to kick his host's dog. He jammed a foot against black flank; the bitch, having devoured one sandwich and with a second in her teeth, retreated obligingly. Alice giggled. Clabburn's footfalls came back along the flagstones. Dr Mack leaned sideways, tidied the moist surviving sandwiches, winked at the children, turned to the door.

"Ah, thank you. The bottle-opener should be in that drawer."

Daddy, daddy, ask him about snakes. Too tired to eat, Alice wanted stories. Orinoco, Amazon . . . Orchids, dugouts, poisoned arrows . . . Dobell caught her pleading look. "Finish your soup, Alice," he ordered, "and eat this," lobbing a russet onto her lap. He turned to his father's old friend. "That python I remember you telling me you once shot . . ."

Some of the stories about being a young medical officer in the trenches in the Great War were hardly for childish consumption. Nor about the terrible night when Sam Mack was home at Abbot's Hall on leave, staying with his widowed mother, and news came that his elder brother had been killed at Gallipoli. Maria Pasqua had wept for her son, she had wept for Naples, wept for Paris, wept for Norfolk. Inconsolable himself, he had tried to comfort his mother; but there is no consolation for such wrongs; slow resignation and slow obliteration are further evils. They had wept, that night, for the young man who would never come to shoot wildfowl on the marsh again, who would never marry, never farm his father's acres, never stroll again in the garden with his slight dark mother who when she was a girl danced so beautifully her mother took her to Rome and then to Paris to make her fortune.

After the armistice, Sam Mack doctored in the Congo, in Brazil. He didn't come back to doctor in Aylsham and farm at Abbot's Hall till he was forty. Maria Pasqua was still alive. He never married. He kept a pack of otter hounds. I wish they'd left us a few more otters, Benedict thought.

———◆———

The python story came to an end. "Have you ever considered medicine?" the old man asked Robert Clabburn.

"No, sir, I haven't. Not really. I want to farm."

"Farming is not enough," the healer of colonists and tribesmen declared.

"Thérèse wants to be a doctor," her stepfather put in.

Dr Mack stared at the skinny silent child. Girls shooting, girls wanting to be doctors, it was all very odd. Still, there had been that right and left. Good luck to her.

"Do you know when the world began?"

"Er . . . I . . ." Thérèse stared back at her inquisitor. He seemed benign – but only just. His eyes glittered under brows that looked like cut-and-laid fences. Awkwardly she glanced at Benedict Dobell in appeal. Awkwardly she addressed her mind to recollections of school science. "Our solar system . . ."

"And the creation of man?"

The demand grated as it came out between the old doctor's yellow teeth.

Jolted by the interruption, Thérèse muttered "Evolution . . ." She felt Benedict's eyes upon her. The trouble was, in her head all she could hear was his laughing voice that had once told her, A weasel is weasily distinguished from a stoat, which is stoatally different – and that wasn't much help now. Still, for his sake she got a grip on her mind. "Mankind developed from . . ." What were they? Then she thought of what they called the elephant-beds Benedict had shown her in the low cliff at Paston where bones and tusks had been unearthed. Imagine when mastodons grazed from the Low Countries to East Anglia . . . She kept at it. "*Homo sapiens* . . ."

"God created the world. Haven't you read the Book of Genesis? And on the seventh day . . ."

Thérèse flushed, looked straight back into the self-appointed catechist's bark face and quartz eyes. "At school I've learned that –"

"You know the stable?" Dr Mack broke in, without concession, without apparent sequence, voice full of nuts and bolts.

"Yes."

Did he mean the one in Bethlehem? To her mind's eye appeared the papier mâché crib with angels, oxen, donkeys, sheep, that Emma took out of the nursery cupboard each Advent, its hundred-year-old blue fading from Mary, gold from the straw.

"There's a ladder to the loft. Go up it. In the loft you'll find a long wooden box. Bring it here. You go with her," he jerked his head at Robert Clabburn, "help her carry it down." The dry bark around his mouth began to crack, the quartz under the cut-and-laid fences shone more brightly still. "Don't open the box till you bring it here."

The girl's doing well, Benedict thought. A right and left of mallard, Huxley to the old fellow's Wilberforce.

Out of doors in the rain, Thérèse felt relieved to be away from that magisterial, barely courteous voice, felt ashamed because she disliked obeying orders given in such tones, felt cold and shivered. Robert grinned at her, they trudged silently.

Willows had rooted in the stable yard, elder scrub obscured the doors. Several rungs of the ladder were missing. The hay-loft was paved with fantails' droppings, barn-owls had nested and left their filth, each swallow's nest had a cascade beneath it. There were cabin trunks with Cunarder labels: Azores, Port of Spain, Rio. Broken wicker skeps, rusty shovels, rotted hay-nets had been forsaken in corners. There were a meal-bin, a Great War ammunition box, two school tuck-boxes that had outlasted the idyllic Edwardian peace when boys were savagely flogged. And there was a long wooden box.

"Our hay-loft isn't like this," Robert Clabburn remarked, whose father had ridden point-to-points, whose declared ambition it was to win the Grand National. "I'll go halfway down the ladder again. Lower the box down to me."

They returned to the fuggy kitchen grimy and wet, carrying an end of the box each. Rain discoloured the dung, chaff and dust on the lid. Dogs were kneed aside, the box was laid on the worn brick floor.

"It's for you, open it," Dr Mack said to Thérèse, winking at her stepfather.

The girl knelt down, fumbled with broken fastenings, lifted the worm-eaten lid. There lay ribs, a skull, femurs. That must be a foot. And that . . . ?

"What . . . ?" She raised her green eyes. "I don't understand."

"When I was at Bart's, I had these bones for anatomy classes. There should be a whole man there. If you don't want him, throw him away."

"No, no . . . Thank you. Sir."

III

Saddling up in the yard at Fen House, Benedict Dobell was happy. Alice looked bonny, sitting chubby and golden on her chubby palomino pony. He had even, by keeping the animal in a stable for several hours every day, stopped the little brute getting laminitis this year, crippling affliction of ponies left to stand in summer meadows gorging on wet grass. The new Arab mare, called Tamara, bought for Thérèse's fourteenth birthday and going out for the first time, seemed tranquil and was certainly decorative, dapple grey with that arrogant Arab head of hers, deep shoulders and arching neck.

Peacocks and fantails were in the yard, pecking up spilt grain. Even the recollection that he had to shoot one of the peacocks barely stained Dobell's peace of mind. Emma was right; a big flock wrought mayhem in the garden; to cull one now and then was good sense and they made delicious eating. Still, it was sad, he was attached to his peacocks, privately rated them above the flower beds they laid waste. He had said he would shoot one and he would do so – but this evening, not now . . . The doomed peahen, a Borromeo White, was not among those jabbing their heads at the gravel, the majority of which were Indian Blues. He put her death out of his mind.

Most of the barley in the neighbourhood had been cut,

some farmers had started on their wheat. The cavalcade
of four clattered along the narrow winding lane under the
oaks in the hedgerows. After another week in his Norwich
office, to ride out through green woods and tawny fields
was peace itself, the blue sky seemed incarnate peace.
He'd always thought to drive a car was a graceless way to
go from place to place. But on a horse he felt good, always
had.

Emma was singing, he rode closer alongside.

Under the greenwood tree . . .

Her green eyes met his blue ones, she smiled. If we just
keep singing, once she had said, this marriage can never
go wrong. Then his guilt that he was her second husband grabbed him by the scruff of his neck. It was a lion, it
swung him up, dragged him away ripping slowly. But
the only result was that, frightened not for himself but for
her, his mind sneered before he could stop it, At least
when she's riding she cuts out the cigarettes for a couple
of hours.

To hell with this idiocy. He frowned at the snaffle with
which Gilles de Nérac's daughter was riding her new mare.
Perhaps he should have given her a pelham, you never
knew, the grey was fifteen hands and an Arab and five years
old, though Thérèse rode well she wasn't strong. Damnit,
yes, a pelham or a double bridle, at least the first few times.

My trouble is, I'm a natural monogamist, Dobell thought.
My marriage makes me absurdly happy, it's all I could ever
want. And it's hell to know Gilles had to be killed for me to
have Emma. Like ghouls of an ancient tragedy, a covey of
fighter aircraft from Coltishall RAF station five miles away
flew low over distant trees. These east coast airfields of ours,
he thought, from which the Hurricanes and Spitfires went
up . . . And Gilles fought for the Free French and I remember myself how extraordinary it felt when 1945 came and
one was still alive. I only wanted to live in Norfolk till I
died, that was my peace. And he had his flat in Paris, in
the Marais, he had his English war-time bride, he had his

peace too. Not that the society we'd fought for lived up to all our expectations. Hell no. And during Suez he would have felt as ashamed to be French as I felt to be English. But Western Europe has been peaceful and free. And having survived the Fascists he helped to defeat, then in a degrading quarrel to be shot down out of French Indo-Chinese sky when Thérèse was so young she isn't certain if she can remember him or if she remembers photographs and tales . . .

They walked the horses down a slope through alder carr, through water-meadow waist-high with rush and meadow-sweet, then over a stream. They trotted uphill between high hedges planted around orchards, screens against North Sea wind-frosts.

"Benedict, can I try cantering Tamara?"

"How's she going?" he asked, wondering why Thérèse always asked him such questions, never her mother. He hoped his wife wouldn't isolate herself too much. The children knew how detached she was without knowing they knew.

"I think she's glorious," Thérèse replied inconsequentially, so in love with the little Arab horse that no evidence of imperfect training, that day or in the years to come, ever sullied her blissful rapport with her mount.

Benedict listened. Marvellous song. That was what England felt like after the war when you could fall in love with no fear of invasion.

> Under the greenwood tree
> Who loves to lie with me,
> And turn his merry note
> Unto the sweet bird's throat,
> Come hither . . .

"Check if your girth needs tightening."

Thérèse cocked up a skinny left thigh in its dirty jodhpur, shoved skinny fingers under the girth. Will she ever put on any flesh? her stepfather mused. Like her mother who eats less dinner party by dinner party, most rakish and least voluptuous of women, still with the figure she had in the war judging by pictures of her first wedding that year when she and Gilles went dancing at the blacked-out Ritz.

"Maybe it could come up a notch."

The girl tucked her riding stick under her right arm, held her reins loosely in her right hand, with her left hand wrenched at the girth buckle.

Here shall he see
No enemy
But winter and rough weather.

Emma Dobell broke off her song. "Combine coming," she said.

Thérèse glanced ahead, pressed her lips together, heaved at the buckle. Roaring and clattering its progress from a cut field to one still to cut, the combine harvester had not yet rounded the bend in the lane. Perched high on his Massey Ferguson elephant, the mahout saw the horses over the roadside hollies and thorns; he put his engine into neutral. Then he recognised them, took off his cap. "Afternoon, Mrs Dobell," he called. "Afternoon, sir."

Tamara had already shied. With a tuneless tattoo of hooves she was escaping backward and sideways, eyes rolling, ears back flat on her skull. The two hunters and the palomino pony stood quietly. Her family saw Thérèse lose her near stirrup and her riding stick at once, then lose her off stirrup, but she was gathering her reins, she was still on . . .

Thérèse had stopped her mare. Fifteen yards down the lane, the grey stood twitching with half-controlled fear. Heart battering, throat trying to swallow, arms and legs quivering, the girl regained her stirrups, urged her horse forward. Her stepfather had dismounted, picked up her stick, mounted again.

"Would you like me to lead you past?"

"*No!*"

"Is she all right?" the driver asked, clapping his cap back on his shining pate.

"Thank you, yes, she's fine."

The engine of terror didn't move; but it blocked the lane from ditch to ditch. Shins and calves sodden by Tamara's sweat, hair and back damp from her own, Thérèse murmured "Come on, it's all right, come on." She kicked her shanny mount into the banked undergrowth.

When she was safely clear, she twisted round in her saddle. Her eyes found Benedict's. She spat in a trembling voice, "*He* asked *you* if *I* was all right!"

"Here's your riding stick."

"Thank you."

"You did well to finish tightening your girth." If he could make her smile she'd have to start to relax. "The best rider in the world can't stay on if the saddle slips off."

"I didn't tighten it." She gave a gasp that was nearly a laugh, but her eyes were still hectic and wet. "I never got the buckle undone."

"Let me."

"No, I'll try again."

"Good."

"And I still want to canter Tamara. Forward this time."

Behind this conversation rode the silence between the war-time bride wrapped in her later detachment, and the child of her second calmer marriage; between a woman one of whose virtues it was that she never performed more than she felt, and a girl who ached for it to be her riding her father appraised. Behind them the combine driver – who like every bailiff and dairyman for parishes round considered Emma Dobell the most glamorous creature North-East Norfolk had ever seen – put his cacophonous machine in gear.

Along a palisade of Lombardy poplars, blackberries were ripening. Beside the brambles, a grassy headland sloped uphill.

"Will this do?" Benedict Dobell asked.

Thérèse nodded, swung her nervous mare off the lane, broke into a trot. The Arab streaked into a gallop; but in a hundred yards Thérèse had reined her in to a rocking-horse canter. She stopped at the top of the headland, proud dapple grey horse (Dobell was beginning to think the awesome cheque for Tamara had been worth it), proud girl glancing round for him under the brim of her riding hat, through those glasses that were supposed not to shatter if she fell.

They waited for Emma. Then for the aged stumpy pony bundling up the headland. Alice was laughing, so excited was she by the brisk gallop, so quickly forgotten were her jealousies. Her blonde pennants fluttered. Her knees and elbows flapped gracelessly.

———◆———

Tunstead church stood among its limes and beeches. Hayseed and pollen drifted in the warm air. Blotchy brown and white Jacob's sheep mooched among the crooked gravestones and sunken mounds, foraged for grass among nettles, thistles, docks. Soon after the church was built, the village had upped and offed one plague year. It was a parish of scattered farms.

Dobell honoured the hallowed places of his countryside, preferably those in decay. He was delighted that Smallburgh workhouse had fallen into ruin; equally delighted that the paupers' graveyard with its nave formed, not of stone, not of brick, but of superb limes, outlasted the injustice its nameless dead had suffered. Likewise he would ride out of his way to pass a chapel an unremembered sect had left, a tiny building of yellowish clay that each winter crumbled more disastrously, its only twentieth-century users a smallholder's bantams. And he liked Tunstead church for its magnificence and its solitude, the five hundred believers it might have held, the half-dozen who turned up one Sunday a month.

Dobell occasionally went to a service there too. The parson liked him to read the lesson. Benedict's contempt for religion was as mild as it was unwavering. His scepticism was eighteenth-century, Hume and Voltaire were his masters. He went to church because he liked the rhetoric and the architecture, the parish ritual so close to desuetude; because he was amused by his own mannerly readiness to jump through the hoops his society held out to him.

So he kept faith indolently with his dead lying under the nave, he reread their memorials. Some had believed. Some had not. Most, he suspected, might have agreed it was of no significance if a man believed this or that or nothing at all, so long as he never talked about it.

Emma had not accompanied her husband to church since their wedding and their daughter's christening. Belief in truth or in love was like fear, she once remarked: no one expected you not to feel it on occasion, but you were to be despised if you let it affect how you behaved. Our marriage is a necessary fiction? Benedict had enquired. None of them are necessary, darling, she had drawled, it's just one we can have if we like.

A knapped-flint porch. A stage above and behind the altar – had miracle plays, Dobell wondered, been acted there long ago? A crypt beneath where Alice – when she had asked her father to hold her pony outside – liked to creep and pretend to be afraid. A fair number of his ancestors, his connections by Georgian and Victorian marriages, lying under the sheep and butterflies as well as under the nave. Yes, it was a satisfactory place, good for musing. To that church, to its surrounding orchards, spinneys, fields, sea-light washed ashore unwarped, suffused his mind with evenness.

"Shall I make you a fence?"

"Yes, please."

Thérèse held Benedict's reins. From the stubble, he could see Sloley church one way, Worstead tower rising above its woods, the round Saxon tower of Beeston further afield but clear because it was down-sun. Natural steeplechase country.

Quickly he heaved bales of straw to make a modest fence for the new mare. Let her jump one fence decently, he thought, and we can call this birthday present a success. The horse is skittish, but she'll calm down, Thérèse will get the hang of her. Again he gazed away over the afternoon shadows on the reaped field. Yes, yes, this was where he belonged. There toward the coast in blue haze shone Honing church tower. Further again – incongruous among mediaeval landmarks – he made out Happisburgh lighthouse, red and white.

He grabbed two more bales by their bindertwine, made a wing for the jump. This was what he was born for. Good. Now then, two more bales, the other wing. Right.

Mounted again, he asked, "Shall I give you a lead?"

"Mmm, please."

She ran her tongue over her lips, wheeled Tamara away, kicked in her heels. I wish her legs came another inch or two down that animal's flanks, her stepfather heard himself think. Oh well, she deserves a horse slightly too big, slightly too fast. She's one of life's overreachers, or I'm trying to make her one. Jumping the new mare could have waited till tomorrow, till next week. No – she's at her finest doing what she can barely do.

Dobell cantered in a semi-circle, saw the girl ready to follow him, Tamara curvetting but under control. He put his horse at the fence, jumped it. The drubbing of wild Arab hooves was lost in the scream of fighter jets low overhead. Benedict looked back to watch Thérèse jump, but he knew everything had gone wrong. The straw fence had no horse near it. Ears back, tail flying, the grey was going a mad gallop halfway across the field.

He watched Thérèse tug helplessly at her reins. Then through dust kicked up by racing hooves he saw she had given up trying to stop the run-away brute; she was just hanging on. Probably she was crying something. He was glad he couldn't hear.

Then it was over. The Arab charged straight at the hawthorns along the lane, looked as if she'd swerve left – or was that the girl trying to pull her round? Anyhow the horse swerved right. Thérèse pitched over her withers.

Dobell saw his wife canter across to her daughter lying on the ground. Feeling sick, his face cold and greasy, he rode over to comfort Alice.

"Wh-wh-wh . . . ?" She stuttered into the beginning of a wail. Bit of a coward, he thought involuntarily. Her face, that was usually golden and pink, was dirty white. Her blue eyes were so wide he was repelled.

"We'll go and cheer up Thérèse. Then you can come and help me catch her horse. That may not be easy."

Alice stared, she sniffed. Tamara was trotting on the far side of the thirty-acre field, head swinging, stirrups dithering.

"Will Thérèse be all right?"

"I'm sure she will. Let's go and see."

That could be a broken collar bone, he thought, recalling one of his own. His imagination, he noticed, refused point-blank to think of Thérèse's neck, her head, her back. Of course she was all right. Still, more than one of his contemporaries lived in wheelchairs because of falls; impossible not to . . . no, think of her wrists . . .

"Nothing broken," Emma said. "You'll live." She dabbed the girl's cut cheek with her handkerchief, wet it with her tongue, dabbed again. "You were doing well. That was bad luck." She met Benedict's eyes as he trotted up with Alice. "She's fine." His face didn't show a thing, but his eyes blazed back at hers. "Look here," she held up Thérèse's glasses. "Didn't even break these."

While Benedict went after the loose horse, Thérèse sat on the stubble and just managed not to weep with her shock, her shame, her aches. It was a dry hard field, there were small stones; her clothes were torn, she was grazed down her shoulder, her elbow, her thigh. They were burning straw in the next field, ziggurats of black smoke plumed up into the midge-speckled air, a smell of conflagration blew across, she heard crackling. Seeing the hawthorns come toward her faster and faster was nothing; knowing she would come off was nothing . . . It was her cry of fear that rang in her ear again and again, that screaming would be hard to forgive.

When her erring birthday present was led back to her, Emma offered to change horses for the ride back.

"No," Thérèse said.

All the way home, she tried to stop feeling sorry for herself and failed.

<hr/>

Alice had it all worked out long before Fen House appeared four-square and white in its trees. Thérèse was all cuts and bruises. Mummy would take her upstairs to be bathed and anointed, bandaged and made much of. Daddy would be left to look after the horses on his own. So he would need help.

She had toted four saddles into the tack-room one by one before Dobell understood what an onslaught of industriousness this was. But then they worked as a team; they carried two bridles, two sticks and a hat each (Benedict and Emma rode bare-headed). Alice led her pony down to the paddock, he led the two hunters. Then he went back for Tamara who was neighing alone in the yard, chucking her pretty Arab head in her collar, tittuping her delicate feet.

The sun was setting behind the west wood. The horse chestnuts that had lost their candles months before, the limes that had lost their flower and scent, the Portugal laurels that had lost their filmy flower, stood with twilight beginning between their branches. Woodpigeons cooed; sometimes one swept up from the tree tops in that way they have, glided down on extended wings.

Benedict leant on the paddock rail, cheroot in hand. Alice clambered onto the lower rail.

"I like horse-watching," she said.

Her father, who had imparted to her both that mode of indolence and that phrase for it, both of which he'd got from his father, said "So do I." He watched the peacocks, picked out the white peahen he must shoot.

All four animals still had sweat-stains in the shapes of saddle and girth printed on their short summer coats. The hunters lay down to roll on the sere grass. Alice squeaked with delight when her pony followed suit, fore-legs buckling first, then hind-legs, then palomino flank tipping sideways, fat paler belly coming uppermost, a heave and four legs in the air and over she went onto the other side, rubbing the itchy sweat off on the ground. Only Tamara, sweatiest of all, stood off nervously, flicked her ears, twitched her tail.

Feeling soft from her bath, her swollen cheek smarting from Witch Hazel, Thérèse left her mother rummaging in the kitchen drinks cupboard, went into the yard. It seemed marvellously unchanged; her fall off Tamara, her scream, might never have been. The rosemary bushes were reassuringly constant; so were the fantails. She strayed empty-headedly. Espalier pears on an outhouse wall were ripening, Doyenne du Comice and Josephine de Malines . . .

Oh but she'd be back at school before it was time to pick the pears! Oh God God damn damn – *school!* Wasps had found one pear they could gnaw into already, that meant the holiday was nearly gone. She stared at a yellow and black head poking from a khaki cavity. Self-pity repossessed her aching body and shaken spirit, her eyes oozed tears. Why wasn't she still so young she didn't have to go away to school? Why wasn't she in France where they didn't have boarding schools? With her mother in the flat in the Marais that occasionally got unlocked and stayed in for a few days, with her grandparents in Gascony . . . Oh for a land of day schools, a free land . . .

Distantly she heard steps on gravel. She turned. Her stepfather came out of the front door carrying her .410, more than weapon enough to execute a peafowl, mash its meagre brains.

Sent upstairs to wash and put on her nightdress, Alice stopped on every stair. The tick of the grandfather clock measuredly followed her up. Tick, tick, tick; then step, baluster; then again tick, tick, tick.

In her sister's bedroom, riding clothes had been flung onto the bed beneath which Dr Mack's long wooden box had been stowed. The future doctor was unsure whether medical school freshmen were still expected to present themselves with skeletons; nearer the time she would enquire.

But she had no intention of throwing the bones away. So there the box waited, like a trousseau.

Alice drifted on beneath the watercolours on the landing into her own room. An ostrich egg mounted in silver. A glass dome enclosing stuffed bee-eaters, golden orioles, hoopoes, beloved guardians of her sleep, feathered geniuses she talked to. Her grandfather's sabretache which he had had made into a folder – Alice was determined to keep her important documents in it when she had some. An alabaster saint from Volterra. A jade Buddha from Macau. A silver betel box from Mandalay. A brass candlestick essential during the power-cuts that never came often enough, sometimes only one a winter. (Unknown to her, the last one had been caused, not by the February tempest bringing branches crashing across lines, but by her father switching off the electricity mains so she could go deluded to bed, glimmering candle in hand.)

Who could wash or change with light so auspicious being pitched softly and silently through the panes in stooks and sheaves to lie strewn like a forsaken harvest all over the tatty carpet and narrow child's bed? Alice curled up on the sill.

Voices rose from the terrace. She peered. Her father stood talking with Thérèse; she couldn't hear the words, but she heard the tones of a masculine no and a feminine yes. After a bit her sister took the .410, left her father standing ill at ease on the terrace, and marched stiffly down the lawn.

There lay the lily pond, lilies closed for nightfall Alice knew, dragonflies gone to sleep. She watched Thérèse jump the ha-ha, walk on getting smaller.

Which peacock would it be? Alice was vague. Oh, that one. Thérèse had loaded one barrel, stood still ten paces from the peacefully pecking bird. On the lawn were wagtails but they were all right, and the mallard on the weedy water too, and the moorhens in the reeds.

Alice wiped her breath off the window. She saw Thérèse take aim, heard the shot, saw mallard rise, wagtails flit away, surviving peacocks climb ponderously shrieking up the dusk into the trees.

Now Emma, glass and cigarette in hand, was the figure on the terrace. Benedict was striding down to the ha-ha. Thérèse stood over the white peahen. The head must be red, Alice thought, and next year I can shoot things he has to shoot but doesn't want to shoot, not her, me, me.

Two

I

Too many people he didn't know. Jolting along bleak lanes
through the moonless night, Kit Marsh had arrived aching
from being wedged into the back of a shooting-brake with
a child that had whined till it was allowed not to go to bed
and a terrier that had whined for fifteen miles. Now he stood
shivering in his duffle coat, stamping his cold feet on church
path gravel.

Mr and Mrs Clabburn he was meant to know, and they
were kind. But these Clabburn neighbours, these car-loads
of Clabburn cousins he couldn't distinguish from Clabburn
brothers and sisters, these Clabburn uncles and aunts, these
Clabburn dogs . . .

Grey figures swathed in coats slammed car doors; sturdy,
spectral, they tramped through the gale shuddering in the
trees up to the glowing porch. Kit followed. Where was
Robert? Not that he knew Robert Clabburn either; he
was in his last year at Cambridge and looked dauntingly
debonair. Kit was vilely conscious that the coming year
would disclose whether he could pass the exams to enter
that inspiring place; but still, Robert was his host . . .

"Where are we?"

"Where *are* we?"

Robert grinned at the boy shuffling into the pew beside
him.

49

"I mean . . . I . . . I can't remember the name of this church."

"Barton Turf. All these muddy villages look the same to you?"

"Oh . . . Er . . . In the middle of the night."

Robert knelt down. They were all kneeling down. Kit thudded onto his bony knees, a prayer book fell off an oak ledge. Eyes open, eyes shut? What did one do with one's hands? What did one think if one was these people? if one was him? Already Robert was getting up. Kit sat too.

"Here." Robert shoved a hassock sideways with his foot. "The stone is cold."

"Oh look! What marvellous figures on the screen!"

"It's lovely, isn't it?" Robert murmured, hoping his guest would drop his voice. "Pity some of the faces have been scratched out. Old dissenting country, East Anglia, old Ironside country. When people get up to go to the altar rail, you'll see the paintings better."

When Kit realised this was his Lord Protector's way of telling him not to be embarrassed if he didn't want to take holy communion, in sudden respect and affection he took Robert to his heart – where, indeed, Robert stayed.

The church was packed for Christmas Eve; the congregation took a long time to be given the bread and wine; Kit dwelt on the rood screen panel by panel, passionately committed those defaced figures to his mind, the faded reds and golds on the carved arches. Contented now, he resolved he would never again be unnerved by rigmarole and piety. That was awful, he must outgrow it. What would his mother think? She would smile. Thinking of her made him smile, sitting at midnight in the nave made gorgeous by candles, by holly and ivy, the solitary figure in the pew, a rank of Clabburns kneeling in the chancel. London and his mother seemed a long way off, his mother whose name was no longer Mrs Marsh (there was a Mrs Marsh, but Kit's father had married her in Muscat, they never visited England), his mother who though she never suggested going to church took him most weeks to a concert or a play. What would George Orwell think, whose books he was reading and

50

reading again? Or Bertrand Russell? They might smile too. Here came Robert. What a beautiful tweed greatcoat he wore.

"Party? What? Oh, yes."

Kit Marsh's contentment was shattered by the pleasantest things. As the service ended, he had wanted to ask Robert if he believed in God or did he come to church because it was a likeable social occasion and to accompany his parents? Trailing out down the aisle, he had wanted to tell the choir how much he had enjoyed their singing, but it never occurred to him he might have the courage to accost one of those surpliced figures chatting gaily by the font. Then the parson had shaken his hand and he had felt embarrassed that the cleric's manner repelled him. And now Robert said they were going to a party.

"Come on, Kit, you can't have forgotten. We're going to Fen House, to the Dobells. Just for a drink. They're old friends, you'll like them."

Who was that girl hurrying away down the path into the night, fair hair whipping out from her hat? Had she been in church and he never noticed?

＊＊＊

Two more miles in the back of Mr Clabburn's shooting-brake. The same terrier, a different nameless child. The car stopped, the hatchback opened, Robert hauled him out laughing.

"Poor old Kit. On the way home I'll go in the back."

Again too many people he didn't know.

Emma Dobell had been drinking brandy with Thérèse while Benedict and Alice went to Barton Turf church. Now, half drunk by the middle of the night as was customary of recent years, but graceful at barely betraying it, she found Kit Marsh standing gawkily in the hall.

"Do take off your coat. Not that I'd blame you for keeping

51

it on. Not one winter since I've lived here have we succeeded in getting this house warm."

Never had a woman who wore so much jewellery, or who smelled so sweet, taken his coat off him while he thought he was still undoing the buttons.

"Th-th-thank you."

Robert Clabburn disengaged himself from his embraces of arrival, ushered his protégé into the drawing-room. There were too many people for the stranger to feel at ease, not enough to make a crowd in which he could lose himself, perhaps thirty all told, of which he knew five or six.

Thérèse de Nérac was the most forbidding. The hand with which she shook his was the slimmest whitest driest living thing he had ever touched. On her stiletto heels she stood six foot and made him feel his additional height was intrinsic unforgivable gaucherie. Her scarlet dress fell sheer and pressed as plywood to her silken legs. Her silk scarf was knotted arcanely round her throat and would never be ruffled because she never moved her head. The shadowy hollows under her high cheekbones looked at him stilly, indifferently. Her green eyes didn't see him at all. (Her glasses she had come to find unbecoming; her new contact lenses hurt and lay discarded upstairs.) She let his warm damp hand fall, went back to talking French to the man standing by her chair, who looked and dressed like a skiing instructor, Kit thought, whose panic had made him malicious, but who was a Parisian surgeon, and Thérèse's lover that year.

Give him Clabburns. Give him their weather-beaten faces, their cheerful talk. Give him the Clabburn cousinage any day, even Clabburn church-going, even Clabburn dogs. Above all, give him Robert.

Happily Robert was always there. Mulling wine was always there too. Emma, Thérèse and the surgeon had their brandy bottle on a marquetry table. (Kit, stumbling away from Thérèse, hanging his head, had liked the inlaid peacocks and doves.) But for everybody else, Benedict Dobell was on his knees in the hearth, jerseyed back bent, firelight flickering on his greying fair head, Burgundy bottles full and empty by his side, a conical brass pot on a long wooden handle balanced among the glowing logs. He mulled wine occasionally on winter nights simply because his father had done so. It tasted of the twenties, of his golden age when his parents had been young and blithely fashionable and pretty wild, when he had been their adored younger child. To Emma, the wine he mulled tasted of the *vin chaud* in cheap Paris bars that had kept her warm that first lonely dissipated winter after Gilles was killed; tasted too of the debauchery that had accompanied the dissipation the next winter when she was going to a lot of parties but still frequenting the same bars, perching her child on benches. She therefore preferred other drinks. They were always stronger drinks. To that child, grown to a svelte young woman, mulled wine was a family embarrassment, something you joked about because you couldn't hope your chic friends wouldn't notice this provincial ritual. And to Kit Marsh, now, it was a refuge. Robert and he took over Dobell's jars of cinnamon and sugar and cloves, his corkscrew, penknife, oranges. Long after everyone had a full glass, Kit crouched by the fire-dogs.

And Alice Dobell? Was that her he had seen vanishing to a waiting car down the miry path from the church? On the far side of the drawing-room, beneath a painting – though Kit didn't know it – of a previous Alice Dobell in old age with a King Charles on her lap, she was if nothing else the only person present younger than he was, and that was something.

Acting as her father's aide-de-camp, bearing to the hearth a cool sticky glass to be replenished with hot Burgundy, Kit saw she had adopted her commanding officer's uniform. A mossy disintegrative jersey flapped raggle-taggle round her thighs and was bundled at her wrists. Over her trousers, a pair of his pepper-and-salt shooting stockings were folded in bulges below her knees and flapped at her toes.

Arrived at the fireplace, she leaned down, held out the empty glass with one hand, held back her swinging hair with the other.

"More," she said and smiled.

Kit turned to the embers, the flames. One sooty fire-brick at the back of the fireplace had something scored on it – a name? a date? The girl in the churchyard had had longer hair, longer. Or was that the wind streaming it out? And now he had taken such care to keep the brass pot and the brazen end of the handle in the fire, to keep the pale wooden shaft from singeing, he hoped . . . And the wine must be hot but never boil . . .

With trembling arms, he lifted the handle, backed the wine from the nudging logs. It jiggled darkly. Would it spill?

"Hold the glass closer."

Had he said that rudely? Probably not, but why did he have to think he had? Would he live the rest of his life nightly playing back the day's vanities and vacuities, longing to rewrite and reperform, trying to stop regret becoming self-hatred? (The answer was: yes, he would.)

Alice held the glass closer.

Kit slid his fingers and palms along the handle which thus, jutting further and further behind his back, rubbed against the varicose veins that had emerged to spoil the lines of Emma Dobell's calves. Why can't Dick leave his bloody dogs in his car? she thought; and, I really must go into hospital for a night to get my damned legs put to rights. Then she looked down; saw the wooden handle; saw the yellow skull and the brown skull bent together, the tremulous purple wine being poured, the green glass held steadily. Emma set her brandy on the mantelpiece with an unkind click, smiled sentimentally down, threw her cigarette past the oblivious heads into the fire.

"Ow!" Alice put the glass down on the hearth with a light clatter, sucked her burnt fingers. "Hot!"

"Sorry."

"Not your fault. These glasses are thick, but they're not thick enough."

Kit picked up an unused glass.

"They look like the bottoms of wine bottles."

"That's what they are," said Emma up by the mantelpiece, making a valiant and unnoticed effort to soften the rasp in her drawl. "I found them in Switzerland, years ago. In Italian Switzerland."

Would Alice stay sitting beside him on the hearth? She made no move to pick up the scalding glass again. But would the fire prove too hot for her? Kit grabbed the poker, manoeuvred log from log. If only Robert didn't come to his aid with more wood, with advice . . .

"Where did you buy such a vast Christmas tree?"

Begemmed with old painted tin candlesticks, old painted tin baubles and birds, it stood twelve foot; the five-pointed star on the topmost shoot almost scraped the ceiling; the vestiges of Victoriana on its inner boughs glistened in dark green gloom, on its outer boughs rubbed against wallpaper and paintings.

"My father and I cut it down in the wood. Quite a business getting it in here, setting it up."

Tomorrow – no, already today – she would kneel under those branches that dropped their needles on the rug. Pale sun would trickle into the Fen House drawing-room at the low, almost level slant of midwinter midday. She would haul out from the stacked brilliant parcels whatever it was she had wrapped up for the man whose privilege it was to axe conifers with her. She would perch smiling on the arm of his chair; she would take his champagne from him so he had two hands to undo his present, she might set the glass beside that vase of Christmas roses on the marquetry peacocks and doves.

While Kit . . . Miserably he brought to mind the two small packages he had brought up from London for Mr and Mrs Clabburn, that now lay among things more amusing and things more personal under the tree at Durstead Hall. Should he have brought presents for *all* the Clabburns? No man could have foretold how many Clabburns would think they had met him before. Oh God, would they have presents for him?

Alice would have parcels too for her cliché mother and worse sister; maybe even aftershave for the skiing instructor. And something for her boyfriend. Did she have one? Yes, probably. Oh why hadn't he realised that at once? Or perhaps there was someone she worshipped secretly, for whom she had either not had the courage to buy a present or for whom she had bought something so inconspicuous her family wouldn't tease her, a present the dullness of which shone with love. Was it Robert she adored? That roan hair. That way of laughing with his mouth shut, his mirth a puff of delight expelled from his nose, as faintly audible as the lines were faintly visible that crinkled round his eyes.

She was off.

"You'll trip," Kit muttered desperately, staring at the thick shooting stockings waggling at her toes.

"Yes, I probably will." She looked down at her baggy camel feet on the Persian rug. "Very useful at Christmas, men's shooting stockings, they hold more presents than socks."

Their eyes rose at the same time, glance in glance.

"Do you still hang up a stocking on Christmas Eve?"

"I'll do anything." She cocked her head sideways, smiled; but the smile at once became a giggle on the lower half of her face, a shyness on the upper. "If you want one of my stockings, take it off. Hang it at the foot of your bed. I'll fill it with presents for you."

Kit had stood up when she stood so he didn't have to address her woollen hip, so he didn't long to bind his arms round her thighs. Down he went on his knees again, but not awkwardly as he had in church, this time with Elizabethan hauteur.

"How will you get to Durstead when I'm asleep?"

The giggle recurred. "On my magic carpet." She stamped one foot. He reached for the nearest shin. She backed away, gingerly clutching the now touchable green glass. "Why do boys only want to play rugby?"

"Goodbye."

Kit got to his feet wearily. If he hadn't said that, probably she would have taken the mulled wine to whosoever it was, come back to finish discussing magic carpets. Never again would her jewelless hands and throat and ears, her unmade-up cheeks be so close.

"Happy Christmas," she said, smiled, turned.

Happy Christmas, he thought. Goodbye, unkissed.

She was going. Why mull wine? Why ever mull wine again? Throw on more logs, knock over the brass cone, spill the stuff, he didn't like it anyhow, his Swiss glass had cooled three parts full. He never considered that the single glass Alice's father had given her had gone to her head. How small she looked, walking away. He wondered where she went to school. A boarding school, that was for sure, he thought, recalling his own grammar school. Thérèse had made him pray he had stopped growing; her half-sister made him confident the great thing about standing six foot two was that he might easily lift her in his arms.

And now – quick, quick, something to do. Logs, the woodbasket, good idea. Where was it? In the window embrasure, behind that fall of curtain? He could pretend to look.

Victorian portraits could be turned to face their walls for all Kit Marsh cared. (He earned his living as an art historian for ten years before he felt more tolerant.) But that looked seventeenth-century and Italian, what was that? Fixing his ephebe's gaze on the six balls of the Medici coat-of-arms as a healthier emblem to honour than the star of David on the dying tree, he wriggled through the crush. Arrived below a murky canvas, he leaned a hand on the wall of the alcove in which it hung. The frame was handsome, though at some stage it had suffered dry rot. The painting was of a Medici tomb – but which one? He began trying to identify brownish mythological figures on a brownish ground. Two fingers inched idly on flock wallpaper.

She had hunkered down beside him on the hearthstone. Then smiling she had said she would come to his bedside. Even now she was in the drawing-room behind his back; she was among the sitting, the standing, those men of stick, women of straw.

She might love him. The jolt of his heart shook his chest, rocked up his neck, crashed his brain against his skull, pressed sweat from his scalp. She just might. It was possible. And if the possibility existed, was a beginning not made?

Yes! Already they had begun! The first minute of their love affair was passing right now, it was just too abstract to be sensed, so frail it was unlikely to survive. Abstract – but now he sensed it. Did she? He sensed it ghostlily.

Never did it occur to him he might not love Alice Dobell, might come to love someone other. It was arbitrary, yes; it was chance, yes; but the possibility was here, was now; possibility was the most real thing in the world, it was the real world. He must turn round, walk in again among the heads and voices, body temperatures, affections, views. Thank you, he whispered to the dun Medici tomb. You did me well. Never did it occur to him that his love or Alice's might be destructive.

"Stroking wallpaper," said Emma Dobell, "is one of the few sensual pleasures one can enjoy in public."

Kit Marsh was already turning to search the party.

"Yes, isn't it?" he said, and greeted her with the most radiant smile that had probably ever yet, she reflected, lit up his thin white face. Certainly many years had passed since any temperate smile of hers had been answered by such joy. Equally certainly his first unease with her, so quickly and weakly let slide into contempt, was gone and could never come back. Was she not Alice's mother?

Alice had vanished.

"Excuse me," Kit said, thoughtlessly phrasing the first adroit sentence of his life, his smile now adult and wry but no less charming, "can we stroke the wallpaper in five minutes?"

"Of course."

He was away. Nobody in the hall. Just coats and hand-bags and scarves piled on chairs; holly and ivy festooned over portraits and landscapes, over the looking-glass, the barometer, pikes and swords. The grandfather clock had been converted to a bower of yew and golden cypress; holly berries were red dots on the faded gold paint on its pinnacles; its tick sounded gently, slowly, under the thud thud thud of his feet. He charged into the dining-room, from which half the china and silver from dinner had been cleared. Into the kitchen where the dirty clutter had been dumped. No one. Back to the hall. I was looking for you, he would say. Simple enough. They would talk of anything, nothing. But possibility would not die at birth. He flung open an oak door.

In the library, Benedict Dobell stood in the glow of one lamp and the fire. He was reaching down a book from a shelf. The swirl of Kit Marsh's entrance made the nearest curtain shiver. In a chewed basket Dusk, who after a lifetime of having his bed in an outhouse had in his decrepitude been allowed to share his master's sanctuary, raised his grizzled muzzle, his nearly sightless eyes.

Man and boy peered through the twilight at one another with equal surprise.

"Oh, I . . . I'm sorry."

"Come in." Benedict completed the lowering of his book. "I'm not really hiding from my guests, though I've been known to do that. My godson Robert wants to borrow this. At least, I've told him he should read it." He tilted the spine to the lamp to check he had the right one. "Izaak Walton – do you know him? Wrote about fishing. Rather well. Robert and his father go to Scotland to fish, he might find time to read this between one trout or salmon and the next."

Kit closed the door behind him, advanced into the stillness. If this man welcomed him with no question as to why he had been barged in upon, he was a worthy father for Alice. Benedict was enfolded in Kit's new seeing that the world was good. His daughter was forgotten.

"What a glorious library."

"Oh . . . You'll find a lot of better ones. But do look if you'd like to." Slowly he was recollecting who this lad was. "You're staying at Durstead . . ."

"Yes. Most of the time, I'm in London. With my mother."

That was right, Dick Clabburn had told him. The boy's mother was on the brink of a third and most unnecessary marriage yet. He was at a loose end at Christmas. Sad. So Dick . . .

"Thank you for your help with the mulled wine."

Kit was eddying about the carpet, homing in on a picture that took his fancy, an old morocco binding that for no reason gleamed more attractively than the rest. Miniatures were hung where shorter volumes left a few inches free. He leaned, gazed. On one high shelf, tusks had been laid. Their yellowing ivory shone. He craned.

Too innocent not to act at once on his host's invitation to scan the shelves, he was also, that evening, too inspired not to be honest with strangers.

"It was something to do. Mulling wine. I felt a bit overwhelmed."

"It was very kind of you."

"I thought . . . I thought Thérèse was terrifying."

"Thérèse is twenty-one," her stepfather replied, as if that elucidated everything.

"I didn't know what to say to her. She didn't say anything to me."

Already Kit felt more benevolent toward that rigidly upright silence, that poised unseeingness.

"She has her London life. Very smart." Benedict Dobell smiled. "Though her mother and I have dined at her flat."

One of his rare delights – along with cutting down a fir with Alice – was taking Thérèse to lunch at his club or a restaurant. He was losing his wife to melancholy. He knew that. He had tried so often to win her back; failed often enough to be getting weary. Melancholy was like a dazzling lover, it triumphed by natural ascendancy, as the not yet discovered will always triumph over habit in a heart with any courage and any pride. Emma's enthralment turned his delight in his marriage to a nagging fear, probably unjustified but quite inescapable, that he was boringly uxorious. But Alice still came to him with a full heart; he was still the man she loved most. And Thérèse was old love at its most gallant: he only occasionally invited her to do anything with him; she invariably came.

Kit was kneeling, making friends with Dusk.

"What does she . . . ?"

"She's at Bart's."

Could that dismissive hand be a healer's hand? After repeated scrubbings with hospital soap, it clearly had repeated rubbings with unguents too. He regarded his own hand on the dog's head, the hand he knew couldn't paint but he hoped might write essays. In the corner of his eye he saw Dobell carry the fire-guard to the hearth. It was a solitary man's fire, three logs from a fallen apple tree charring together.

"You must take your book to Robert."

"I think I should."

Side by side they drifted away from the Manton flintlock on the chimney-breast, past the Chinese jar full of potpourri.

"Did you inherit these books, or have you collected them?"

Kit's ease was so new he didn't know he had it, this wonderful ability to declare what he felt, to ask what he would be interested to know. For the rest of his life it came and went, alternating with anxiety. But that night it had come for the first time, hadn't yet gone for the first time.

"Oh, about half and half, I should say."

"Your library is a very peaceful room."

Benedict Dobell thanked him gravely. Above them, the heads of two antelopes looked down over tablets reading Transvaal with turn-of-the-century dates.

"I hope you'll come back. If you're in Norfolk at Easter, ring up, get Robert to bring you over for dinner."

"Thank you, I will." His voice lilted. "I will!"

And Alice, his heart recalled, back at the oak door, I haven't asked about Alice and now . . . The jersey Benedict wore was as voluminous and ruinous as the one he had bequeathed her. Kit dropped his eyes. Yes, below the knickerbockers were just those stockings.

Benedict, holding the door open, saw in the brighter light

from the hall a first suggestion of unshavenness on Kit's lip, hair that needed washing, eyes no particular colour.

In the same brightness, Kit saw a Tiepolo etching he hadn't noticed before. He checked like a pointer finding game. It showed Death reading from his book, a few people listening for their names, a dog as ancient as Dusk and less well fed, ribs staring through its hide.

"Oh . . ." Kit breathed. "It's brilliant." Any other night, he would have been ashamed of such simplicity; but not in that aura Dobell unwittingly shed. "Is it Domenico Tiepolo?"

"No, it's Giambattista, actually."

The hall had filled with people putting on coats, with voices saying goodbye, with cold from the front door standing wide. Robert he must find, and quickly. Hadn't there been something he wanted to ask him earlier in the night? Yes. But he couldn't remember what. Anyhow that could wait. He had a more vital demand.

Kit dodged past knots of Good nights, Happy Christmases, hugs. What was the rush? None. Utter. Intolerable. He hurried unaware past Alice waiting to say Goodbye.

In the drawing-room, Thérèse was alone, sitting on an ottoman, lighting a cigarette. When he saw Robert wasn't there, Kit swivelled in the doorway, ducked back into the tumult under the mistletoe, grabbed his duffle coat off a chair, bolted outside.

"Good night, Kit," Emma Dobell drawled and held out her hand. "Thank you for coming. We'll keep the wallpaper."

"Good night. Do you know where Robert is?"

"When the yard looked jammed, people parked in the orchard. One car is stuck of course. I think he's helping push."

A cold wind scoured the gravel, rattled through hedges and fruit trees. High up against cloud-rack, oaks and ashes jerked.

Kit plodded over sopping grass toward headlights and reversing lights. He slithered in a boggy patch, his shoes filled.

"Look, I know this isn't a good time to ask . . ."

Robert Clabburn straightened up from the car he was heaving.

"For heaven's sake, ask away."

"It isn't the right thing to ask either . . ."

"Here, push. What on earth – ?"

"But, oh, do you think there'd be any chance of your parents asking me to stay again?"

"Yes, of course. Come whenever you'd like to." Robert laughed his quiet laugh, his laugh utterly without irony. "Which of my girlfriends have you fallen in love with?"

"Wh-wh-what about Easter?"

"Easter? I'm afraid we're going to Greece."

II

"What shall I do?"

"Jump aboard," Robert ordered. "Then do whatever Alice says. I'll hold *Bittern*. You've done a bit of sailing, haven't you?"

"A bit. Crewing. Not much."

"She won't let you take the helm." Robert Clabburn laughed his quiet laugh; this time it was silent, lost in the flapping of many sails; but the skin around his eyes puckered into crow's-feet. "If you can be a willing crew . . ."

Kit Marsh teetered where sea lavender gave way to shelving mud; he waded into incoming tide. A hand onto a shroud, his hip onto lurching gunwhale, he heaved himself aboard. The boom swung; Alice reached to shove his shoulder down but reached too late; it clouted him across the head.

"Bad luck."

Robert handsome in fisherman's blue cotton, sunless Whitsun wind fluttering his hair as it tattered the marsh scrub. Robert as handsome as he was in his jockey's silks standing in the paddock at race meetings, listening to owners' and trainers' counsel, too relaxed to flick his boot with his racing whip. Robert the cynosure around whom the less charismatic clustered on the bank of the creek as they clustered round him in members' enclosures, at cocktail parties . . . Or so Kit had no doubt, though he went to no cocktail parties.

The boom swung back; he ducked, fingered the bruise coming up on his temple. Was his ear cut? Yes, rusty smudges came away on his fingertips. What a mess it must look.

Robert who would push *Bittern* off for Morston regatta, stroll back along Blakeney creek to where among the faster boats his own was waiting. *Whirlwind*, a creature of glistening woods, of tapering alloy mast, of sails as white and spreading and altogether exaggerated as a wedding dress. *Whirlwind* of myriad controls – incomprehensible to Kit – in sequences of ropes and wires, blocks and cleats. *Whirlwind*, creature of wicked moods and of wild speed. *Whirlwind* who belonged to a class called International Fourteens . . . Kit Marsh was hazy about classes, though he had delighted Robert by saying that, judging strictly by appearances, these were clearly the Steinway Grands of racing craft.

Robert Clabburn who had been born with acres, with stocks and shares . . . Kit was hazy about them too. And preferred not to take them into account.

"Cley to port, North to port." Benedict Dobell, who eight years before had triumphed in the Battle of Morston Creek sailing in his old-fashioned way in cavalry-twill trousers and a tweed shooting coat, stood on the bank wearing the same trousers, the same coat. "Then South to starboard, Mussel to starboard."

"Cley to port, North to port, South to starboard, Mussel to starboard," Alice repeated the buoys after him.

"Then Pit to starboard."

"Mussel to starboard, Pit to starboard . . . Then North again?"

Benedict's voice carried through the battering of the sails of the waiting fleet; but she had to yell to be heard, it made her feel stupid and shrill. She wished her father were crewing her rather than Kit.

"That's right. A run back to North buoy. Mind the gybe. You'll have shipped a lot of spray by then. Running back, you can get Kit to bail."

Alice nodded, her face eager but wan. When the race started, her stomach ache would go. When she got out on the harbour, she'd find the course instinctively. She smiled at her father, but her lips were pressed tight, her smile didn't work.

Kit caught her eye, the blood bumped in his throat like a pile-up of dodgem cars at the fair. Soon, soon, they would leave the shore, they would be together out on that choppy grey sea. She too longed to be away – but he knew that was because she longed to get racing.

The starter fired the blank cartridge in his sixteen-bore. The first, slowest boat set forth.

"North to starboard."

"North to starboard."

Catechising can be a form of love, Dobell thought.

"If the wind gets up and you don't feel like gybing round North, remember you can tack round."

"Yes." She swallowed. "Then South to . . ."

"North to starboard, South to starboard, home. Leave the post at the mouth of Morston creek to port."

"North to starboard, South to starboard, home."

As boats pushed off, the remaining vessels were walked down the creek toward the start. Sitting in sopping clothes with your feet in muddy bilges and your head wincing when a boom slammed across could be a form of love too, Dobell thought, watching his daughter's would-be beau.

"Kit," he said.

The boy started as if he'd forgotten some order.

"Y-y-yes," his teeth chattered.

"They sailed from here to chivvy the Armada. Cley creek, Blakeney creek, Morston creek, they were all wider and deeper. You could sail up the Glaven to Wiveton in those days, where now it's marsh and water-meadow. A few ships put out of Cley to chase the Spanish north."

"Tomorrow I want to explore!" Kit ducked the boom and yelled.

"You can walk over the harbour bottom at low tide this afternoon. Get Alice to take you."

"And go to churches!"

66

"I think you might like Cley church," Dobell called through sails suddenly slatting louder in a gust. "And Salthouse is handsome."

"Are the rood screens good?" the boy's shout came back.

"You're next!" Robert cried to Alice. "Oh come on," he grinned at the starter. "*Bittern* away, surely. The helmsgirl is getting cold. So is her crew."

The starter consulted his clipboard, consulted his stop-watch, consulted Alice Dobell's hair blown to obscure her tense face. He smiled. "Off you go, my dear."

Beating into the westerly wind down Blakeney Pit, at the tiller she was free of stomach cramps, free of all care. She had first sailed these inhospitable waters before she could walk, when in her carry-cot she was regularly lifted aboard *Trio*. Cley to port, North to port, South to starboard, she murmured the buoys gaily now. *Bittern* and the other slower vessels were tacking round North buoy before the starter released the fastest boats to follow them. *Whirlwind* wouldn't catch her for a long time, let Robert wait and see.

"Ready about. Lee-O!"

That was all Kit heard from her. Time and again. He let fly one jib sheet, flung himself across the hull, the foresail flapped its way past the mast, he hauled in the other sheet. Flooding tide swirled around the fishing-smacks moored in the bay, rumpled brown and noisy at their chains. Shouldn't Alice give these perils a wider berth? Maybe not, but . . .

Landward, Blakeney church diminished among its trees and clouds. It had two towers, a bell-tower and a lighthouse-tower. Cley windmill still held up four white skeletal arms, but the sailless ghost grew tinier. Seaward, among the dunes on Blakeney Point, the redundant lifeboat-house, sand hillocks long come to block its slipway from the tide, huddled in the blear wind.

Here came *Trio*, slashing through the jumbled troughs and crests. Benedict no longer raced, but he sailed. Now he had come out to watch his daughter race. He was single-handed; he usually was these days. Emma was so listless, she did less and less of anything. Thérèse had not been up to Norfolk since Christmas; probably she would

67

not return till it came round again. Alice was better, he believed, at the helm of her own boat. And he . . . *Trio* still delighted him. Her brass cleats that always needed polishing. Her ancient mast, known locally as 'that sorry stick' after a mocking remark of Dick Clabburn's – but it hadn't broken yet. Her bowsprit that struck justifiable terror into incompetents who sailed out onto the harbour and got in her way. Her various leaks, all of which had been caulked repeatedly, and opened again whenever she went out in a stiff breeze.

"*Trio!* Daddy!" she shrilled.

Benedict raised one hand. "You're doing well," he shouted.

Gaff creaking, bowsprit plunging at the seas, spray scending, *Trio* went seething by.

"Isn't she beautiful?"

It was the first conversation Alice had initiated all race.

Kit couldn't tell which of the sails on the harbour were racing. He couldn't tell which competitors were Muck Boats. With courses laid at weird angles to the buoys and to the wind, he couldn't tell who was leading.

Bittern rounded Mussel, a wave broke at her veering bow, spindrift crashed over Kit's head. He paid out jib sheet, grabbed the centreboard to heave it halfway up.

"Jib!" yelled the girl his dreams of whom had been a tormenting distraction through months of studying for his A levels.

What? Oh, it was flapping. He yanked it in a bit. His hands were stiff and sore.

Bittern reached sturdily through the waves humping into the harbour mouth. On the windswept sand spit of Blakeney Point, grey shapes lay.

"Are they seals?"

Alice shook the twisting hair off her mouth and eyes, caught his glance, smiled at him. One hand on the helm and one on the mainsheet, she could indicate nothing; but with her eyes she gestured overboard.

Kit's mind filled with her smile till his brainpan couldn't contain it, the smile burst forth, it reappeared on his face

68

transfigured into a halfwitted grin. Then he stared at the sea alongside. A dark grey head stared back. It looked like the head of a big sodden dog, with sleek hair, with contemplative eyes.

"Lots of them!" she called happily. "I love the seals. I've always loved them."

The seal pack was lumbering down the spit into the surf. From the mightiest bull seal to the smallest pup they flippered their ungainly way through drying starfish, razor shells, bladder-wrack. Over them the blazoned black and white chevrons of oystercatchers whirled on the grey pelting wind. *Bittern* lolloped by; around her, more heads broke the surface.

"Oh . . . !" Alice suddenly wailed. "*Has* it turned?"

"What?" Why did she have to switch so treacherously fast from delight to misery? "Has what . . . ?" He had failed to keep his irritation with her out of his voice.

"Has the *tide* turned?" she spat, raging at herself, at the sea.

They gazed around. There was nothing, not an anchored yacht, not a harbour mark, close enough to show flood or ebb.

"Perhaps it's slack."

He spoke without conviction; she heard him without respect.

"Have you got a watch?"

"No."

"Nor have I." Her father never wore a watch; but it would have been enough for him to scrutinise these chaotic troughs and crests, he would have known which side of Pit buoy to lay his course. "We've got to overtake *Avocet*." She wriggled into a less uncomfortable position on the thwart, blinked spray from her eyes. She wasn't tall enough to wedge a foot against a leeward strake; sitting up to windward made her legs ache as infallibly as helm and sheet tired her arms.

"Which is *Avocet*?"

"The only one still ahead!" Really he could be damned stupid. Hadn't he noticed how thrashing up the bay she had overhauled all but one of the slower Muck Boats, had not so far been overhauled by any of the swifter ones? She heard flapping forward, yelled "Jib!"

"What about this one?" Kit demanded as a vermilion spinnaker swept tranquilly by.

"Not a Muck Boat. Doesn't matter. *Avocet* matters." Here was Pit buoy. "Stand by to bear away." Would it be a gybe here? No, ahead *Avocet* was running east still on port tack, the gybe would be at North. Port tack! She must remember to give way to boats beating up on starboard. Alice glanced over her shoulder. None of her rivals were hard on her heels yet. But they would be. "Come inboard. Get the plate up." She bore away round the buoy. Which side of the orange cask lay the turbulence? The wind pitched waves at it from the west; but there was lesser turmoil on the east side too, a foaming ruff that meant the ebb had begun. When the tide set upwind in the harbour mouth it would be rough; secretly she was glad she and *Bittern* were heading for the sheltered Cley end of the bay. Robert would have a wet ride in *Whirlwind* . . .

Kit stooped; the scoop scraped on floorboards, strakes, ribs; he filled it with spray they had shipped – spray that had burst aboard in stinging cascades, now slopped to and fro, colourless, spiritless. He chucked it over the lee gunwhale, ducked to the bilges once more.

It was quiet with wind and waves astern. Away to port the dunes slipped by. *Bittern* ran peacefully on an even keel.

Kit gave up bailing. After half a year, Alice was so close now. Impossible that he would not touch her soon. One day! Perhaps today. Impossible that she should think of tides and sails forever. Sooner or later he must come into her mind; she would ask herself what she felt; she would answer – what?

There was her left hand cramped onto the mainsheet, her right on the tiller. His own hands were puffy from water, pinkish blue from cold. He uncurled one painfully. Flaps of torn skin dangled from his palm and fingers, raw flesh oozed, smarted. She wouldn't want to hold his hand.

Oh but she would! Cuts didn't matter. She would know

cuts didn't matter . . . she who glanced continually up to *Bittern*'s gaff and burgee, ancient mainsail wrinkling at the battens, curling at the leech. She would share his longings and his fears . . . she who now gazed longingly ahead past *Bittern*'s forestay to *Avocet*'s transom and the shortening space between, gazed fearfully astern over *Bittern*'s wake to the sails of *Sea Pink, Scandal, Vanity,* crowding down the harbour after her.

Soon he would hold her in his arms. At some unknowable time, it would come. Anyhow after this silly race was over. Her hair, her cheeks, her lips must be salt. Oh why must they wait? It was now he wanted her in his arms, now far from land, far from people, far from the deathliness that lay all around his mind but couldn't invade the centre where Alice was. But *was* she established in his being where she could not be removed? How could he tell? The curve of her chin to which his eyes kept turning, the slant of her cheek-bone – part of his destiny, really? And if so, by what mad combination of chances? And did such vague fortuities determine him so inescapably? His head throbbed. That crack the boom had fetched him before the start. He fingered the pigeon's egg under his hair. Christ, his ear! Caked with blood. No, she wouldn't want to kiss him.

And yet, and yet, to sail a slow battered dinghy on grey sea beneath grey sky: this was bliss. This rocking, this creaking, this splashing, on and on and on. Nothing ahead but the love to come. Nothing behind but the forgetting of all else. A tern tilted past the sails on its swept-back pointed wings. Kit shivered; his drenched clothes were clammed to his skin; salt was drying coldly in his hair. Ever to do anything but sail on like this would be a darkening of counsel, a loss of grace, a –

"Try goose-winging that jib."

"Goose-wing . . . ?"

"Goose-wing the jib!" As her irritation escaped her she grabbed it. "See if you can set the jib to port, the other side to the main."

The wind had shifted dead astern. With mainsail set to starboard and jib to port, goose-winged *Bittern* stole up on

Avocet, drew alongside. Alice's stomach cramped mercilessly. White-faced she stared at her flag and mainsail so as not to gybe unawares, dry-mouthed she whispered to her vessel, Come on, oh come on!

The helmsman of *Avocet* smiled, he called encouragement. Kit grinned and waved on his commander's behalf. More cut off from words and gestures than the seals, Alice gybed round North buoy in the lead, heart thudding so she could hardly breath.

North to starboard, South to starboard, home.

"Plate down," she gasped. "Jib in."

Something else, something she'd forgotten, what was it? Oh yes, the post off Morston creek. To port. Don't cut the corner.

A beat back. A long leg on starboard, a short leg on port, back onto starboard, the last board maybe or would they need another? Where was South buoy anyhow? Must be hidden behind an anchored boat. The ebb was with them now. It was against *Scandal*, still running east but catching them, catching *Avocet* right now, catching . . . Alice pressed her knees together. The ebb might help *Bittern* west just enough before *Scandal* turned and it helped her too; then in the creek it would be against *Bittern* first . . .

In a welter of taut sails and spume, *Whirlwind* came surging by. Having started nearly last, Robert was now nearly first; he was crossing out boats' names in his head one by one like the angel of death scoring out names.

"Well sailed, my darling," he shouted. "You'll thrash them. South to starboard, remember!" Kit stared after *Whirlwind*'s glamorous wake. How could you tell what people meant when they said darling? Perhaps everyone at Cambridge said it all the time. "Remember the ebb." Robert's voice echoed back. "There won't be much water in Morston creek!"

To run aground at this stage! Alice felt tears jab her eyes.

Never had Kit known himself so banished. Banished from a heart where he had never lodged, could never enter. A heart of which he could know nothing, to be understood wasn't what hearts were for, they had other purposes, one day maybe he'd find out what his was, yes, there was a problem all right, better tackle that. He was left with Alice's cheeks pink with an excitement she didn't share with him, her eyes that kept swinging past him without seeing him as she tried to work out when to tack to clear an anchored fishing-smack and fetch South buoy.

"Ready about. Lee-O!" Then a second later, "Jib!" she shrieked.

He had snatched to free the jib sheet from its cleat; but it had jammed. *Bittern* turned through the eye of the wind; the jib was caught aback; she started to lay over on her ear, water flopped over the lee gunwhale. Kit hurled himself at the cleat. Alice flung her helm over again, let fly the mainsheet. Frightened, furious, for the first time ever she screamed "*Fucking hell!*" If this idiot was going to capsize her now . . .

Kit yanked the jib sheet free. Head to wind, sails flogging, *Bittern* was losing seconds. He backed the jib, slowly they got sailing again. Sweating with wretchedness, he bailed.

When the bilges were dry, Kit raised his head. The entrance of Morston creek. Soon this farce would be over, he'd go back to London, he'd never see any of these foul people again. Moored craft. A huddle of figures on the marsh. Boats hauled up on samphire. A post with a Union Jack.

A shot with a sixteen-bore.

Did only winners get a gun, or second and third too? Alice shook with doubt. *Scandal* hadn't caught her, she was crossing the line now, damned close race – but had there been another Muck Boat she hadn't seen, far ahead? She twisted her head this way and that. *Trio* lay at her mooring. Benedict had stopped furling sails, he stood upright and still, he was smiling. Oh Daddy, she breathed. There lay *Whirlwind*, others too; but none of them rivals of hers – she'd won! – Robert wouldn't be waving like crazy if she hadn't won . . .

"Stand by. Lee-O!"
Bittern tacked.

"Did we win?"

"Yes. I think so." She grinned. "Sorry I screamed at you."

"That's all right. Stupid of me."

"No. It was the cleat stuck."

"I should have noticed."

"Where can we come ashore? Is there a gap?"

That stretch of creek year in year out was the home of half-a-dozen craft. Only for an hour this one day of each year was there a flotilla of fluttering sails.

In the ring of neighbours and friends in sodden clothes who stood shivering on the marsh, Kit was the only outsider. He had never looked around at a scene so desolate: mud slopes from which scummy tide was slithering away, miles of browns and greens and blues smudging into one grey.

"First over-all." A grin. "And not for the first time. *Whirlwind*. Sailed by Mr Clabburn. Here you are, Robert."

Clapping. A silver challenge cup was presented to Robert and his crew.

The second cup was picked up off the marram grass.

"And the Muck Boats' Cup." The broadest grin of all. "The real Battle of Morston Creek. As you all know. *Bittern*. Sailed by Miss Dobell. Come on, my dear, you've done well."

Alice stepped forward. She turned back, took Kit's elbow shyly but firmly. "Come on, you too," she said. He followed at her heels.

What did the flatness of the marsh portend? he wondered, islanded momentarily beside his beloved in the ring of oilskins and smiles. What could this wide emptiness portend?

———————◄•••►———————

Sitting beside Alice during the loud cheerful lunch party at Morston Manor, he still felt islanded with her. He prayed

74

nobody else might observe what a wild chaotic ocean all around isolated them from the rest of mankind. Doggedly he listened: Mr and Mrs Dobell, Mr and Mrs Clabburn, Robert and his crew – these were stock markets on which no wealth still moved but which went on registering phantasmal ups and downs, went on issuing reports.

He picked up one goblet, read the list of names. Yes, Robert and his boat had been inscribed before, this precious metal would return to Durstead Hall like an habitué of the house. He picked up the other. *Trio*, Dobell. And now the new inscription would be *Bittern*, Dobell, as soon as it was taken to Holt to the silversmith. It might be the slowest race in England; but in her salt-drenched mud-splattered way Alice had triumphed; and he, however incompetently, he and no one else had helped her.

This is our islandedness! that was what he wanted to tell her. Gaily, twisting the cup by its stem, "Your name will look good here," he said.

His grin met the side of her face only. Across the table, she held her father's gaze with hers; he was smiling into her smile.

Oh, of course. Kit's pleasure stiffened horribly on his blush. He clunked the silver goblet down. It wasn't his. It was with Benedict she shared her race, her cup, her delight. Benedict whose name was already cut into that bowl, who had already lifted that stem, drunk from that lip. Benedict who had taught her to sail, had bought her *Bittern*, to whom she now brought her tribute home.

Kit Marsh bowed his anguished countenance over the débris on his plate an instant too late. Dobell had seen him – pitied him? Kit didn't dare look up; he missed the smile with which the host tried to include the guest in his contentment, tried to give Alice back to her friend.

But he heard Alice give herself back.

"I'm sorry they don't put crews' names on the cup."

"I nearly sank you."

"Very good for me. Do you want to wade across the Pit at low tide?"

When Mr Balding could no longer go afloat, sail-shed

swallows made their nests in his sails, just as Shakespeare says they nested in Cleopatra's. Then he died; another farmer rented the manor meadow for his Ayrshires. The sail-shed fell down. A new sea-wall was built.

Now six inches of brown brack lay in the creek. Wind rapped halyards against the masts of boats lying on mud slopes. Again Kit was alone with Alice. Again he wondered at this land so nearly sea that the sky was nearly as vast as a sea sky.

They crossed liggers over empty creeks, trudged along slimy paths, jumped pools amid sea lavender, splashed through mire. Still no sun. In the grey driven wilderness overhead, he couldn't even see a paler patch where the sun must be. Legs soaked for the second time that day, he shivered as he trudged.

Where was she leading him? This country that barely rippled up from the North Sea; this summer westerly that cut like a winter easterly; these screeching gulls: all were hers, not his. The evenness of ground over which they wandered, the evenness of light that circled them – here if anywhere solitude lay, freedom lay, here if anywhere *égoïsme à deux* . . .

Fording Morston creek, Kit sank to his knees in mud, lost a shoe. He stretched out a flailing arm. She laughed, she grabbed his hand and pulled. His blisters hurt. Still, she didn't seem to mind holding his welts and flaps. She excavated for his shoe, prized it up, flung it out of the creek. He floundered to a moored crab-boat, held on for support, hurt his hands afresh on barnacles. Reorganised on the marsh, Alice wiped her muddy hands on his jeans. He wiped his on hers.

She was on hands and knees tussling like a puppy; the next moment she had jumped up, she was walking on north toward the sea. Kit followed. There her hand swung by her wet leg, why didn't he take that hand in his? When he had smeared filth off his smarting palms onto that thigh, why hadn't he put his arms round her waist?

She strode blithely; she glanced to left and right; it was half-term, she was happy to be home. She breathed salt wind deep, deep; she had won her race . . . Was being with him a fraction of her happiness too? Kit stared at her forehead, tried to decipher the yellow tresses blustering there, saw a C, an S, a Z, an L – it made no sense. People could be so nonchalant, so free . . .

Blakeney Pit had shrunk to a quarter of the expanse of water on which they had sailed. Here was South buoy, lying now in a shallow weedy ditch. Alice sat on it, drummed her heels, jumped down.

Up to their thighs in slack tide, then out on a bank. Kit marvelled at the sea-rippled sand, the lustrous green of weed splotched here and there on yellowness.

"That's the Hood."

Alice pointed across a channel to scrub on a low dune.

"The Hood?"

"It's meant to look like a hood. Don't you think it does? And that's the old watch-house, where the coastguard used to be. But no one goes there now. It's ruined."

"Can we cross here?"

He stared at gusts ruffling the channel. Was that a shoal where they could wade?

"Not unless we take off our clothes and swim."

Was she mocking him or seducing him? Both probably; and probably neither whole-heartedly. "Bit cold," he said before he could stop. No – she was simply explaining it was too deep to wade.

"Further east. I'll show you."

"And beyond the Hood?"

"The sea. Can't you hear it? Sometimes in onshore gales the waves break so high you can see them over the shingle bank."

Kit no longer wanted to kiss her. It was not her hair on his cheek he desired, his lips on her cheek, his lips on her lips. He wanted to have kissed her. Then this anxiety would be past. So then they might kiss again – another time, whenever, it didn't matter, a second later, next year, in another world. The first kiss he would not feel. He knew that now. The first kiss would not have existed. Later, he would be able to say truthfully that it had never been, this sequence began at two, so substantial was his mind and so abstract the world, so much more intense and therefore so much more real his mind than his lips or her face.

"East or west?"

"West," she said. "We can lie in the dunes. Later we can blow back downwind."

Anything to stop her waiting to be kissed, break this waiting that would end with her despising him. Was she waiting to be kissed? No, because it was merely his longing that suggested to him she was. Yes, because the random violence being done to his soul would not let him stop suffering so quickly; he was not to be saved by her rejecting him; this possession had hardly begun to rot him yet and had a long way to go.

Kit grabbed Alice's hand and ran.

"That's east!"

She dragged him round. Their feet grated on stones. They galloped upwind. Down into the foam that blew ashore. Down off shelving shingle onto hard wet sand. Down into the rinsing retreat of the last wave.

Ahead the jumping surf stretched off-white between confused dunes and confused North Sea.

With a roar, the next comber fell. He must have brushed her face with his, because with this dragging splashing cold around his legs the awful hand that had gripped his brain relaxed. Peace came. It was all over. He grinned.

The thunder of falling water changed to the grind of stones sucked back down the shore. Then it was quiet.

Up the beach out of the débâcle, out of the sluicing. He recollected that the cold hand he clutched must be somebody's. He was not alone. He turned. Her hair and jersey were soaked. He forgot to look at her face.

Was this a beginning? Skin shuddering, teeth rattling? Beginnings occurred ceaselessly, was this one anything much? Already it was passing, it was too late to understand. And what could begin in such an unkissed kiss, in such inexistence?

Was Alice happy? Did she think there had been a kiss? He gazed at her, comprehended nothing. A voice of hysteria screeched: Look at her face you fool! see if she's angry!

Why didn't his eyes work? Or was it his brain? He felt his greymatter knot in fear, the mysterious hand was reaching for it, he would feel that grip . . .

Always one had to begin again. He put his hands around her waist. She came toward him, she raised her face.

His mind unclenched.

III

Did the tides bring her peace? Alice Dobell questioned the late summer sun reflected off Morston creek onto anchored hulls. Did each tide when it rolled a mile inshore and rose twenty or twenty-five or thirty foot bring her peace – and then when it ebbed miraculously leave its peace unwithdrawn in her head?

That would mean it was no accident that toward the end of the holiday there should be flood tides: these marsh tides over thirty foot that obliterated creeks, submerged bushes and liggers, were only kept out of the village by the sea-wall. Of course. After modest offerings of peace, these last days gave abundance.

"Come on," she said. "We'll have to wade."

Most of the marsh was already six inches underwater, and the tide was still an hour from high. She took Kit's hand, they splashed forward side by side, iridescence shattering at their shins.

Ditches and potholes were patches of brown. Areas of sea lavender were a purple glimmer. Posts of jetties showed the edge of the creek. A vessel had been moored on a warp too niggardly for this generous tide and was beginning to duck her bow. It looked like a form of torture, Kit Marsh thought – a hull tied fast to what would finish it. But Alice shrugged: if fools didn't know how to moor, to hell with them, she wasn't going to waste an hour rowing from boat to boat putting them right.

When they reached the first ligger over the first tributary creek, they had to wade thigh-deep. They inched their feet along slimy planks sunk in flood pushing inland, inched their hands along the rail. Then Kit barked his shin on the grey fluke of an anchor cutting the flood.

At the second ligger over the second creek, Alice could still feel the marsh tide filling her head with peace. She hadn't slipped and fallen (Kit had). The glistening sea in her mind tilted its planes of light, played its sails and sea-birds within the walls of her skull. She felt the tide rise between her cheekbones, up to her temples, it murmured in her ears. She carried her head carefully; she balanced it high and upright on her neck – holy vessel brimming with sea. Ridiculous – but she knew her shoes wouldn't slip on the mud. Ridiculous – but the tide was up to her eyes. Looking inward (her eyes could do that now) she stared along the dazzle of salt sun on calm sea. Looking outward, it was the same. Above her eyes, the dome of her head was the blue dome of heaven.

"Look, Kit, a skua."

"What?"

"A skua. They're terrorists. Look now."

A black-capped gull had scooped up a fish; it rose into the morning brilliance; a dark hunter harried after it. Kit and Alice shaded their eyes with their hands, squinnied to see the silent fight that was no fight. Mercilessly the skua chased the gull. In vain the victim jerked about the sky; it was too slow, too clumsy. Then terror undid all control, the fish was thrust from the gullet of the gull. The skua dived for its prize.

"Impressive, eh?"

"Yes." Kit nodded, swallowed. Somehow his bile tasted of fish. "The skua never touched the gull."

"No need." She was dumping sail-bag and food basket into the tiny scow the Dobells and Clabburns sculled to their moorings when the tide was in. Usually it lay high and dry on marsh. Today it was floating.

"Hand me those sweeps."

"Sweeps?"

Still he saw the tormented gull, hooded black as if for execution. The demonic skua shadowing it, never letting up, preying on more and more fear. Then that sickness of despair, the fish falling through the air.

"Kit." She grinned. "Those oars you're carrying."

Bittern and *Vanity*, *Trio* and *Sea Pink*, lay to the swirling tide; the light southerly air was not enough to turn them. Alice rowed the dinghy. Refracted warps slanted angling down to chains and weights. Ripplings and chucklings skirmished along planking.

Sails hoisted, mooring cast off, tender left on *Bittern*'s buoy, slowly they ran out of the creek; slowly the wide expanse of water widened still further. Kit was vague about what was deep harbour, what was overwhelmed marsh. But Alice would know. She would steer. And if they went aground – who cared? They could push off, sail on again.

He wedged the jib sheet under one foot; hitched up on one elbow to keep his bony shoulder off the thwart; lolled his head on the gunwhale. That was unpleasantly hard, he cradled his head in his free hand. Oh this was pretty fine . . . The mainsail even shrouded his eyes from the sun. He forgot the skua and the gull.

His leg got pins and needles; he manhandled it across the thwart, hauled in the fluttering jib. Then the blood stopped flowing in his elbow; he massaged it gingerly, propped himself on the other arm.

As for time to come . . . what of it? To Stiffkey foreshore for lunch – if any shore remained above water. And after that . . . Exams – which these days he felt he would pass. Christmas in Norfolk . . . With any luck he would be invited either to Fen House or Durstead. Or perhaps Alice would come to London; he wanted to take her to theatres. Then Cambridge next year. Alice might come to Cambridge too later. Half asleep, Kit had no doubt they would agree what form the adventure of life should take, just as – so innocently in love was he – he had no doubt all moments in one another's arms would be enchanted.

He yawned, he shut his eyes. Lulled by the motion of sailing, drowsed by sun, what lazy arrogant boy would not dismiss all the world except his love as the gross and the crass? The lives of others – their earning and spending, their coupling and decay – what tedium, how unimaginative . . . !

In Venice with his mother in April, he had found a Mary Magdalen by Giovanni Bellini, one head among three painted on a small panel of wood, that ever after was his image of Alice Dobell: an *alter ego* of hers he housed for her in his mind; a surrogate for him to adore – the wide look in whose eyes, the ornament at whose throat, made him dizzy and speechless. But it was love – if love had the nerve to glory in itself alone – love that would illumine the whole world and if it were extinguished would put out the world.

Thus exalted, Kit fell asleep.

Fading astern in the east, Cley windmill held out four dead-white and dead-still arms, empty frames through which the weathers blew, useless spars round a mill that never turned. Alice wondered when it had last ground corn, that ghost with four arms, or a crucifixion with raised arms and splayed legs, or what was the Hindu or Buddhist god with four arms . . . ?

South-east, Morston was vanishing. All summer long, the air in the flint and red brick manor had tingled with her passion and Kit's. Often they were left alone there. Then the low old house with its rattling windows and creaking stairs was the sanctuary of their touches, kisses, whisperings. In its walled orchard they had lain together in the grass till desire became unbearable. Up to its attic they had climbed hand in hand. There among its watertanks and rafters they had shyly helped each other undress, lain down on her truckle bed. (The other, abandoned for years by Thérèse, stood shoved in a corner.)

No one had ever imbued them with guilt; their instincts were not salacious or craven. Like her lover, Alice never doubted that to love and to make love was good; that it was to be hoped for, to be achieved, to be delighted in. "Have you ever done this before?" giggling she had asked. "No.

83

Have you?" "No." "I expect we'll be brilliant." "Mmm, so do I." Only, it was odd, when Benedict and Emma had driven into the yard that evening, she had gone to meet them at the door under the honeysuckle and had felt like the mistress of the house welcoming acquaintances.

Freedom was difficult, but she was learning. The devices of freedom were so rickety. There was the antiquated and nearly powerless motorbike that since her birthday she had been allowed to drive off fields and tracks and onto the Queen's highway. But it kept breaking down. There was *Bittern*; but she too was in her declining years, irremediably slow, given to breakages. And there was Kit . . . but he too – what was it? she wasn't sure . . . but he could be so absent he hardly existed, so racked by anxieties she had to mend him, get him going again.

"Here are your seals."

Kit had woken up, had wanted to give her the first things he saw.

"Yes." She gulped. "Oh . . . Our seals."

One look at him and she wanted to touch him. But she had made herself too guilty.

The seals were all around *Bittern* sailing out of the harbour now misshapen and stretched by flood.

<hr/>

Turning south toward land, heading back against the millions of gallons now ebbing out to sea, they saw the usual land wasn't there. It had fallen back hundreds of yards. In its place spread shallows glimmering blue in the sun.

Not easy to find Stiffkey river. The shoal offshore between Stiffkey and Wells, that most tides was a maelstrom of breakers, lay calm and deep. Far away, the red roofs of Wells village gleamed. Foreshore woods seemed to grow out of the sea. But to hit on the mouth of a winding stream amidst all that inundation, that evenness . . .

Bittern tacked inshore, relinquished by seals, handed on to redshank and stint. They sailed in over mussel beds, then over samphire. The light breeze died. At each tack, the heavy under-canvassed old vessel made less way. Ebb sluicing off marsh, babbling and glittering for miles around, would sweep them back to sea . . .

Alice lowered her sails. "We'll have to row," she announced.

When the blades of their oars dug into mud, Kit waded and dragged the boat. When with a slither, a shout, a splash, he vanished underwater, they had found the meandering channel. Alice hauled him aboard over the transom. *Bittern* drifted seaward.

"Where would we fetch up?" he asked.

"Oh, Denmark I expect."

They grabbed their oars again, rowed till Kit was warm.

Anchored upriver by the drowned tideline, he took off his shirt and let his thin white body be rubbed with a muddy salty towel. They ate their bread and cheese and apples. Around them, the marsh emerged from its waters. The rushing tide returned to its declivities, flowed out down its daily courses. Scrub sparkled with moisture. The larks that haunt the marshland flew back over their restored wilds.

"Shall we walk to Cabbage creek and swim? There's a deepwater pool there even when the tide is out."

"Yes." Kit shivered. "All right."

The idea of swimming gave him gooseflesh. The idea of Alice with her shirt off bewitched him so he would have swum in the White Sea when it thawed.

As the tide went down, two or three baitdiggers appeared with their buckets and forks, trudged out over exposed flats to dig their tumuli. Kit liked no one to intrude on Alice's tidal, reflecting world. It was her sea half land and land half sea. It was her watercolour sky with no hills to spoil her sunrises and sunsets, to take any richness of light from her air. Now more than ever he was anxious. Would anyone else have come to Cabbage creek? Would Alice undress? But he was lucky, their solitude was absolute.

Low overhead, British fighters from one airfield and

American fighters from another howled. They glinted across pale blue wash heaven, ploughed through white blurs of cloud, headed out over the North Sea. As they crossed the coast-line, left hamlets, copses, harvest fields, fumed their vapour over shipping lanes, they accelerated. To the lovers sprawled on sodden tussocks, their flinching faces relaxing as the worst of the scream died away, sonic booms echoed back from sea.

When evening came, they went to rejoin the seals, walking where they had sailed. To the west, translucent bars of cloud flamed and charred. Drenched sandbanks shone in streaks of rose, streaks of mother-of-pearl. Inland in haze, in harvest dust, plumes of smoke towered from fired stubble. It grew cold.

A mile out, Alice dropped onto the sand, wriggled forward pretending to be a seal, stalking a resting pack. Kit watched her creep to within a few paces; saw the bewilderment of one seal turn to agitation among six, among ten . . .

Alice lay still and watched and smiled and longed to be a seal. But something was wrong. When twenty or thirty seals had shuffled away, when their heads dotted the harbour mouth, one remained. She didn't approach it; she didn't want to frighten the sick animal more than she already had. But it was sad. Not all seals were free. Her eyes filled with tears. The seal heaved feebly. It couldn't escape, couldn't help itself; it wouldn't live long, a few hours till that night's tide came in.

She walked on north. In ruffled sand where the pack had been, shadows began to smear. The rusty carcass of a ship and its stranded green buoy threw shadows. Further off lay another pack of seals, their greys darkening.

Shoreward, the baitdiggers had filled their buckets, shouldered their forks; dim and black, they trudged back to land.

She reached the flat sea. Brindled sky was greying like an old dog's muzzle. Kit splashed through the last rivulet, came beside her. Her blonde hair was losing brightness, her face looked white.

It wasn't enough to laze the day away – suddenly Kit

was sure of that. It was so obvious in that hush – why hadn't he known before? He didn't want to laze his love away, he refused! He must stop that happening, it was not too late . . . Alice deserved a higher end. He must achieve a higher end with her. There was more he could give.

"Alice," he said.

Never had he been so awake. In the dimness he saw the wading dunlin more sharply than by day, heard the lap of ripples fall quivering in his mind. More vivid than ever she had been to him, she turned. She raised one grimed hand, shoved her salt hair off her brow. In her damp shirt she was shivering. Her breast rose and fell softly. Her throat swallowed. A muscle at her temple stirred faintly, whitely.

"I . . ." Kit wavered. Ah! – but what? A voice in his head intoned, You are more beautiful than anyone. Another voice remarked, Let the dog see the rabbit, and laughed. "I love you more than I can say. I'll love you for ever."

"No," she whispered.

He didn't understand, she looked triumphant.

"No . . . No." She spoke more clearly; knew what she meant more clearly; saw him more clearly in the dusk.

"Wh-wh-why . . . ? Alice, I only . . . Wh-wh-what is it?"

In his misery he blushed red.

"I'm in love with you Kit – oh yes! But I feel free, I'm too free." She laughed quietly. He heard devils yammering. "I want to be too free." Her low voice rang. "Right now, that's what I want above all."

For what was peace if it didn't make her free? A headful of tide . . . And what could love be if it didn't make her more free momently?

She took Kit's hand, smiled at him, led the ghost stumbling beside her back toward the land. Soon it would be night. Already the sky was dark blue. Soon the next tide would come rolling in at their heels. There must be a first star already – where was it? She gazed west and upward. Yes, the evening star.

"I'm in love with you now." Again she laughed softly. "I'll probably be in love tomorrow too. But after that – who knows?" Why did he have to be so solemn, so stricken? "And it's not the essence."

"I think it's the essence," Kit mumbled tearfully.

He hated her holding his hand. The summer had been wasted. Worse – a mockery. Oh God what a fool he was. Self-hatred kept the blush sweating on his cold face.

"It's not the vital thing."

Damn her, she had forgotten him, she strode smiling through twilight. Why should he answer her? She was talking to herself, to her vainglory.

"Or if it is . . . Perhaps moment by moment. But only that. Kit, do you understand?"

She stopped, swung round to face him, she held both his hands. But why wouldn't he meet her eyes? He wasn't listening.

"Moment by moment, Kit, like now. And for the rest – who cares?"

THREE

I

Raw daybreak at the beginning of the year. Blood-orange sun clearing leafless alder carr, glinting on waterlogged field and lawn. Lane fouled by sugarbeet lorries. Winter wheat sprouting green, a covey of partridges feeding.

Benedict Dobell shivered crossing the yard, Zampa his young deer-hound at his heels. He no longer shot enough to need a gun-dog. Aesthetic considerations alone, after the demise of Dusk's son, had made him buy a deer-hound puppy. No other creature could look so handsome following at his horse's heels. Zampa's beauty was such that she enjoyed princely luxuries denied to the serviceable breed of labradors; she was allowed into the drawing-room, so heraldic did she look lying on the hearthrug.

Hay-nets and buckets of feed for the horses. Grain chucked down for the peacocks and fantail pigeons. An apple from the apple-loft for Benedict. Nothing for Zampa.

"Come on, Zampa, let's go and plant some trees."

The cold and darkness of night had not been dispelled in the outhouses. His dog's exuberant devotion was such that she kept getting between his legs and tripping him. Two brace of pheasant hung from a nail in a beam. Hafts were lengths of shadow, tines and blades gleamed softly. Drums of paraffin, rolls of netting ... Where were the plastic sleeves that saved the whippy stems of saplings from assault by rabbits' teeth? Next shed? Dobell took a spade, a clasp-knife and a hank of cord. He latched that door, unlatched the next. Zampa charged ahead of him into murky wheelbarrows, skeps, mowers, ladders, crates. Here were the stakes he had cut. Good. He took a dozen, he'd come back for more. The rat poison and the spoon bound to a stick were high up out of the reach of children and even out of reach of gambolling deer-hound whelps. The sleeves. There they were. Right. Children – there were no children any more . . . Well, maybe grandchildren one day, maybe Kit and Alice . . .

The ship that carried Thérèse would be docking at Felixstowe about now. She would drive her car ashore, drive up through Suffolk, into Norwich, out into the country again . . .

Every winter he planted trees, just as every year he cut up and carted back to the yard trees that had fallen or died; he kept his wood-sheds stacked with seasoning timber, his fireplaces supplied. But the finest thing was planting trees. To order saplings from the nurseryman; then to carry them down to the wood with your dog frisking, mallard that had spent the night on pond and broad and stream scattering skyward and away. Thereafter to know that in the thickets his young oaks and limes, yews and hollies, beeches and hornbeams, horse chestnuts and Spanish chestnuts were flourishing; that as ancient trees decayed and fell, new vigorous ones were coming up, strengthening the woodland, making it more diverse, more beautiful. To walk by the drive or the stream and see trees growing that he had planted five or twenty-five years before. Every spring to watch them come to life in their ordained succession – except there were uncertainties . . . Heaving his gear across a stile, he laughed, remembering an old rhyme according to which, watching the trees bud, you could foretell the spring's rain.

Oak before ash, splash;
Ash before oak, soak.

Brown wind rasped through boughs. Under clumps of laurel and holly, the earth was dry: here birds beleaguered by foul weather sheltered. Stream and ditches brimmed to their banks. Dead trees rotted into the sodden earth. By the silted duck-decoy, where shingle hard-core had been put down in the last century, it was firm underfoot; beeches grew well here, and rhododendrons. There was another dryish area where once a cottage must have stood; you could sense foundations; dog roses and other remnants of a garden grew. But further down the fen toward the broad, in the pulpy land only alders would grow, and the marsh orchids that sprang up every May.

Dobell found a sapling planted the winter before that had died; he replaced it. On he moved through the brumous wood, planting where time and gales had destroyed. To choose a place, looking up to check the young tree would not be overhung. To dig. To kneel, to settle the roots in black soil, press the loam down with your fingers. To stake the little tree firmly, knot the cord, cut it. To stand a moment watching your dog fossicking in undergrowth (Zampa squirmed and whimpered puppyishly, looked not at all heraldic) before you pushed on . . . These pleasures had often stood him in good stead. But now with Emma ill . . .

Why should sunlight appearing and disappearing through cloud be a presage of anxiety? But it was. Five minutes of effulgence, five minutes of gloom. Rain spitting, then stopping.

Thérèse must be nearly home, perhaps she was turning into the yard right now . . . No, no, he wouldn't go back to the house till he'd planted all his little trees. They needed to get their roots into earth; any night the frosts might bite below the surface, the weather for planting would be over for the year. Poor Thérèse! To drive from Paris with her heart full of dread; to drive back with her dread more vivid. To come back whenever she was free until one time not even the ghost of Emma would be here to put her brittle arms round her daughter's neck. He would stand alone to meet Thérèse when she drove into the yard. Alone with his dog, that adjunct that gives solitude the appearance of loneliness. But it would not be so. He had been solitary these last years, so completely had his wife retreated into her dejection, her lassitude after drinking, her indifference. He had learned how not to feel lonely – not very, not deeply. It was his guilt for not suffering his impending bereavement more acutely that was the most cruel thing Emma caused when she betrayed him with her melancholy.

Benedict rested on a stump. He must write to Alice in Rome, she must be made wretched too. No, no, no sitting down to think! He had three saplings still to plant. The wet mud on his trousers made his legs shiver. North-east wind gnawed through his lichenous shooting coat. Three more holes to dig. How would it go? Dear Alice, your mother has been in hospital for tests . . . He stumbled over a mouldering branch.

This was more or less where he had reckoned the last of his little trees should go. He looked at the three living twigs in his hand, three magic wands, tiny lime trees with reddish purple buds, with scruffy earthy wisps of root. Yes, here trees had fallen, here was a gap in the covert. Let there be three magnificent lime trees. Let the lovers of the next century and the century after that come here and kiss and hope for enduring joys. At least he would undertake that there should be lime trees under which the kissing and the hoping could proceed. He laughed, frowned, stared round at the tangle . . . where was it . . . ? Hereabouts, he'd forgotten, but yes, hereabouts, when he was a boy he'd kissed – who had it been? Benedict had no time to wonder, in his head he heard Emma drawl: Alice, darling, I've got cancer, stupid of me isn't it?

Three holes, three trees, three stakes. Pick up cord and claspknife, don't forget the spade. He straightened his stiff back. No, not lonely . . . solitude was a virtue, luckily one he happened to have . . .

His knife fell through the torn lining of his pocket. Absently he fumbled for it. The knife fell through a tear in his coat lining too. He saw the bone handle on the frost-withered brown stalks. That was how his wife had gone, for no good reason, inevitably . . . She had dropped through tear after tear, fallen away and down until . . . This was silly. He picked up his knife, laid his spade on his shoulder, set off toward the yard.

People of ordinary carelessness left one for a new love. But Emma was too poised for that, or she'd had enough liaisons before she married him, or she was too contemptuous of herself. Once she had told Benedict she was wobbling on the brink of a love affair. But then she had pulled back from it. When he had asked why, she had told him she couldn't tell the difference between having an affair and not having it. So then he had understood how inert their marriage was.

He snorted with bitter laughter, trudging through swamp and brushwood, through renewed rain. How shocked he had been! That was where years of giving all his heart and mind had brought him. Emma's uncaringness was so profound she didn't have to hide it; it hid itself beneath her flawless superficial dedication to her husband, her children. So unconvinced by passion had she grown to be, that she could deny it to herself without regret; she let others pretend to delight another, fail to be delighted. So unconvinced by love was she, that she couldn't even want to stay alive for his sake or for the girls . . .

A car with French number plates was parked in the yard. Tramping by the greenhouse, Dobell saw the letters had been delivered. He pushed open the glass door. In summer the greenhouse was sad: musty air, empty shelves, cobwebs, bluebottles, void. But in winter he liked it. Now involuntarily he smiled at the banked greenery. With momentary oblivious joy he breathed the mingled scents of the delicate plants flourishing in their sanctuary. They were themselves the arcanum, their mortality contained the essential secret, like the sibyls. Or they were voluptuaries at an upper window while an army marched beneath, men and women whose nervous failings happened to be the only veins of peace in that culture still being mined, whose weaknesses were the temporary behaviour of instincts of inestimable worth. He admired the lemons on the lemon trees. He rubbed a leaf of scented geranium between finger and thumb, held it to his nose. He glanced at the writing on the envelopes; his faint smile took stronger hold. "Hey, Zampa," he murmured, "a letter from Alice! You haven't met her yet. But come and meet Thérèse." Zampa wriggled, she kettledrummed her paws, she wagged her tail, a watering-can was knocked over.

———◆◆◆———

When Thérèse had arrived she had found nobody. In a pier-glass in the hall, glass foxed with brown blotches like an old etching, she saw the small black bats that had attached themselves beneath her eyes. Not much sleep in that cabin bunk last night. That is what she would say. But the bats roosted there most days; only at night they took wing, when she left her hospital, bathed, put on her finery, made-up her eyes, went off to a party. "Benedict!" she called softly. "Emma!" No reply. She lugged her suitcase up the stairs, chucked it on the bed beneath which Sam Mack's box of human bones still lay.

In the drawing-room over the mantelpiece hung one of those round convex looking-glasses with which previous centuries increased the light cast in a room. The carved sea-horse at the top had been a benevolent genius of Thérèse's childhood; she paused to greet it. The convex glass took her small fine head, made it broad, thick-boned, cretinous. It made the window opposite look tiny and far away. In it, a mote moved. Who was that, diminished, warped? She turned. Her stepfather was walking along a hedgerow, carrying something slanted on his shoulder, heading toward the house. Beside her ticked the Boule clock he wound up each week because he liked its tick, but that successive experts and tinkerers had failed to make tell the time. She was attached to that clock: it also had begun its life in Paris, though two centuries before her.

In the kitchen, her mother had materialised. But no more

spectral than usual. Good. Emma Dobell was disassembled by the dresser panes, put together by them patchily, shakily. Her hair had been just this grey last year, it was no more discoloured. Her thin mouth had turned down at the corners for years, this was nothing new.

She advanced toward her daughter, held out her arms. As she came, her foot caught on an uneven pamment of the floor. "Bloody thing." She kicked, grinned. "This house is falling to bits. Like me."

In her embrace, Thérèse smelled rain on Emma's hair, Guerlain on her throat, what was it on her hands, saddle soap? Difficult to distinguish smells, the whole kitchen was fragrant with the hyacinths on the sills.

"Have you been polishing saddlery?"

"Yes . . ." If that drawl were ever to speed up, things would be seriously amiss; but it was as slow as could be desired. "I'm pretty lazy. But sometimes . . . the only thing I want to do is spend hours playing the piano . . . or fiddling around with the bee hives . . . or polishing saddlery. Then I go back to my feebleness." She was hauling bottles out of the drinks cupboard. "What do you fancy? It seems we have sherry . . ." She peered. "Pernod. Gin." She set them on the white table of scrubbed beech. "Do you like my earrings?" Up went one ringed hand to push back her lacklustre hair.

"Yes, I do." They were emeralds. "Where did they . . . ?"

"The harness chest." Emma laughed. "Among racing boots, hunting boots, saddles, bridles, rugs, girths, surcingles, bits, a mass of old stuff. Someone going away and afraid of thieves had hidden one of her jewellery boxes there. Benedict's mother probably. We'll see if he recognises anything. She must have forgotten where she'd hidden it. And none of us searching for things in that chest . . ."

"What else is in the jewel box?"

Thérèse was getting ice from the fridge.

"Oh . . . Quite a pretty amethyst brooch. A moonstone bracelet. I'll show you. Bits and pieces. A platinum necklace – they liked platinum in those days. Take anything you want. You can have these earrings one day." She laughed. "Quite soon. In a year or two. Perhaps less."

Thérèse felt ice strike through her palms.

"Emma . . ."

For an instant her mother regarded her straight, spoke straight.

"I do apologise for this disease. So unnecessary."

"You haven't changed." Thérèse smiled waterily. She heard her own shoes click on the pamments, heard the rattle of ice she flung into the sink. "Just don't ever change."

"Change . . . ?" Emma drawled her laughter. "No . . . I shouldn't think dying will change me at all . . ."

With a crash of iron and oak, Zampa bounded in from the yard. An icy flurry of air, a spatter of rain, barking. Benedict Dobell followed, stamping his boots, shoving the door shut behind him.

"Shut up, Zampa!" He took off his cap. "Thérèse. Welcome home."

A hug of decaying tweed. Would he remark on how scrawny she was? He must be used to thin women by now. Only Alice had a little flesh on her bones, not much . . . Alice fornicating happily in rented rooms in Trastevere . . . Alice sitting on a café terrace on midwinter spring mornings of Roman sun and birdsong . . . Goddamnit, Benedict was thin himself. Good to hold him, though – very good. Thérèse stood on her toes, reached to kiss his cheek again. At least he'd learned never to remark on how early the drinking began.

Alice's letter was opened, passed from hand to hand.

9th January
La Fosca, Urbino

Dear Father and Mother,

Kit and I have come to grief. I mean, he's left me.

We had gone to Arezzo for a few days, for a New Year holiday. He said he didn't want to be with me any more, he wanted to live alone, independently. For him this is a marvellous new beginning. He thinks he is transcending our love affair, he sees a life of freedom ahead of him. To

98

me it seems a blank end. I can't imagine not loving him.

I have not been very good at thinking what to do. He went back to Rome, to work. I took the bus to Sansepolcro. After three days I came on here. My money is running out. Probably I'll go to Milan – the agency I modelled for in Rome said they could give me more work there.

I'll write and tell you where I fetch up.

Love, Alice.

All the short winter day, the cattle in the field waited. Then in the afternoon a tractor and trailer appeared jolting over hillocks and tussocks. A farm labourer with a pitchfork tossed out kale. The cows straggled, heads down, along the line of food.

Chimneys in the neighbourhood began to smoke beyond woods and meadows, windows began to glow through bare boughs. The rain drew off, it was cold, perhaps it would snow, the sky was that brownish slate colour. Blackbirds pecked at fallen apples in the orchard grass.

Dyspeptic from drinking too much at lunch, Emma Dobell stood at her bedroom window. On the lawn below, Benedict and Thérèse separated, set off with guns under their arms to take a covert each. From the sluice between the lily pond and the broad, a heron rose into the air, flapped its ungainly way over the alder carr, trailing its spindly legs.

What should she do? She'd mucked out the stable. What did one do when there was nothing to be done? One wrote a letter full of love and consolation to one's daughter in Italy . . . but she had given no Milanese address. Well, for another week or two Alice would be spared knowing of her mother's further withdrawal from her.

Thérèse had vanished into blustery woodland. Emma saw pigeon fly upwind over the tree tops. A strong wind kept them flying low and not too fast: probably there'd be game to pluck that evening – the very notion exhausted her. Thérèse would pour drinks and talk cheerfully and help pluck birds and – oh God what ennui . . . Tales of her medical career, her Paris nights, her Mediterranean holidays . . .

And Benedict, where was he? There, walking some hazel thickets in case pheasant were drawing in off the open land now day was ending. Benedict with a new worry now, going in among the trees, swallowed up. Benedict who would want to send Alice money – which he wouldn't have much of to spare now he'd decided to stop working. Who would have liked Kit as a son-in-law, who already thought of him as such, who lent him books, talked to him about pictures, passed him his box of cheroots after dinner. Who would dwell unflinchingly on the image of the girl weeping in cold shabby bedrooms in Sansepolcro or Urbino or wherever. While Emma could dwell on nothing; her mind flinched even when it wasn't hurt. Nor was it, she added scrupulously, capable of being hurt to the degree that her husband was vulnerable.

Benedict heard wings, a cock pheasant rose over the nut trees. He swung after it, missed, saw it again between two thorns, shot it with the left barrel. Without a retriever, it took him a couple of minutes to find it in the undergrowth.

Choosing a place to stand for pigeon, he wondered where in her spinney Thérèse had positioned herself; there were two or three possible places in a north-east wind. It wasn't just to Italy it was hard to dispatch one's love and be sure it was felt there. He couldn't even love inspiringly enough for it to have much effect on the doomed woman in his own house. Perhaps as far as Thérèse under her shuddering lattice his love could be pitched, could reach and be felt to have reached. He wanted to talk to her. Perhaps that night she'd join him in the library . . .

He didn't believe Kit had fallen out of love with Alice; Kit wasn't like that. But what would Thérèse say to that idea? Here came a pigeon swerving through the feathery heads of Scots firs. Benedict raised his gun too late; it was gone before he got a shot. He hoped Kit in Rome wasn't feeling too miserable imagining what was being thought of him in Norfolk. If he was more in love with freedom, good luck to him – though life might prove difficult.

Pigeon. He missed with both barrels. What was this suspicion in his mind? Thérèse would help him focus it. Something about how Alice was happy loving, she believed in it, she was good at it. He missed another pigeon. This was getting ridiculous, he must concentrate. He reloaded, stared at the rim of his patch of sky where the shadows came into sight labouring into the gusts. The only thing was . . . what if this wasn't just lousy bad luck for Alice? if it was the origin of an unending waste, if she never fell out of love with Kit, not truly?

He must ask Thérèse. Crack. Missed. Crack. At last. He picked up the warm, blood-bedabbled bird. His shot had cut open its crop, he could see grain just eaten, not yet digested. Then if Alice in future years came to love someone else and married him and bore his children – still she would have given her finest love before and so would Kit – idealists both of them, as Benedict had been – and that love could not be given again. When would the snow come? It must fall soon out of a burdened sky like that; in from the sea it would drive, pelting on cliffs and marshes.

Hadn't more pigeon flighted when she was a girl? Anyhow all that had come so far Thérèse had missed. That was the trouble with only shooting once or twice a year, she thought, and some years not even once. That was the trouble with this indoor Parisian life – how could she expect not to be out of practice? As for winter sojourns in Biarritz and Cortina, summer weeks in Sardinia . . . These were more obvious, more common pleasures than standing shivering in a wood with a blizzard blowing at dusk, if pleasure it was; but they helped not at all, what she needed was an hour shooting clays.

One ash tree had tilted against another, the two trunks groaned. Squalls bundled into the thickets. When snow began to scud, it whitened the north-east sides of trees, scurried on mud, disappeared in the brown waters of ditches, melted on the barrels of her twelve-bore that a few shots had slightly warmed. She looked at her fouled tattered shooting mittens – Sam Mack had worn mittens in the same condition – at her well-kept painted finger-nails emerging from them, and laughed.

She missed two more pigeon, then killed three out of the next five. Practice. She liked their grey shapes swooping over the trees, twisting in to roost. She forgot the cold. She enjoyed her accuracy coming back.

When the pigeon stopped, it was time for duck. She trudged with her game-bag down to the water-side. Benedict had already left his covert; he was standing under a screen of willows. Where should she stand? That clump of silver birch over there had provided cover for duck-flighting in the past; she'd be half hidden but she'd command a span of sky.

This was more companionable than standing in different woods. Up the slope, the lights of the house gleamed beyond the trees. Her stepfather looked very alone, standing there among the lifeless reedbeds in the white swirling gloom. Well, she'd come and be with him sometimes, they'd stand for wildfowl . . .

There was a time when the sky was pale and the water dark. Then, as evening dimmed, the shades were reversed, the water was paler than the air. But now snow was confusing everything. Oh let them come soon, the first skein of wild ragged shapes that would see the glimmering water and circle round high above, would gather confidence, circle again, then come whirling down. Mallard, teal, let them come, come soon, or even with these contact lenses she wouldn't see to shoot.

Was that them? Yes! Their voices! High in the weltering snow, somewhere, somewhere, she heard their soft quacking, their colloquial talk. Would they flight in here to feed or would they go winging on to other ponds and broads and streams? Oh come down, she breathed. Was that a flying mallard? No, a twist of driven snow dusk . . .

Emma closed the drawing-room shutters, drew the curtains, put a log on the fire. Why was she so weary? Time was she had rejoiced in snow. A shot carried to her on the wind. She sat, doing nothing, hearing time drip from the clock. Even death . . . Death would eliminate the real, what little real there was, but it would leave the unreal, leave all this . . . She smiled at the battered eighteenth-century Boule, the face that showed the wrong time. Another shot. Quietness.

II

"Back!"

Alice put the horse-box into reverse.

"Straight back up the loke!"

In one mirror, Zampa was sniffing a nettle-bed. Alice twisted, craned. Where was her sister? In the other, a flowering hawthorn, a patch of blue sky.

"Can't see very well!"

If she flung herself far enough out of the window to see directly behind the horse-box, she could only reach the clutch with a ramrod left leg and a quivering left foot.

"Straight back, Alice!"

These voices, these echoes. Still, good to be home. Ah! there was Thérèse, those lanky legs of hers (my frogs' legs, she called them) in breeches, that green shirt, that black hair, walking backward, beckoning. The horse-box juddered, nearly stalled. Alice trod on the accelerator, took her foot off the clutch before it fell off it, heard hooves behind her on timber floor.

"Stop!"

"Bit further back, I should say."

That was her father's voice. Her mother, of course, had no opinion; she stood, she waited, didn't even pat the dog.

The trouble was – would anybody else want to get a vehicle up this loke? Judging by the length and straightness of the grass, probably not. Alice jumped down from the cab. The trouble was – these voices . . . what were the people they came from? Who were these habits of perception she called her family? these patterns of behaviour neither her own nor independent of her that with familiarity she loved and could sometimes predict? And why did their voices, just by being voices, all remind her of Kit Marsh? Just because he had come to be an incomprehensible infinity of words and gestures, couldn't anyone else yell Back! or Stop! and have any being in yelling it?

Months after losing him, it was getting worse, not better. And everyone was tired of her turmoil. She herself was stupefied with tiredness. He made less and less sense, he'd come apart; and that meant there were so many Kits to say Goodbye to.

There was the Kit who wouldn't recognise this horse-box (it was new); another who knew the one before. The Kit who had ridden one of the horses and been fond of it. The Kit who would not recognise this bracelet but who knew her wrist as well as she did – better, probably, he was more observant. It was endless. And each Kit who separated himself from all the rest had to be lost individually. Some hours she was assailed by losses, torn apart, the marauders made off in different directions with different griefs of hers. Other hours there was only one, she felt lucky; one grief she could get to know, indulge in, start to enjoy. Asleep, if she dreamed, there was this love or that love to lose afresh; or if she didn't dream, she didn't suffer, but didn't know she wasn't suffering, so it was no relief.

And why did he have to have taken all words to himself? The shit! the shit! she wailed to herself, striding round the back of the horse-box. Scowling hard to stop her face wincing, Alice flung herself at the bolts of the ramp. Not one word she remembered him using – not a word or phrase he must have used – might be uttering now – might one day think of – but for a moment it was all of him and therefore all her love and all her grief and hopelessness. And though some moments were gone fleetingly, others lasted an hour, a night, still others looked like lasting all her life. Why wouldn't the bolt undo? She swung all her weight off the ground, the bolt turned, she cracked her elbow on the iron rim of the ramp, stumbled away nursing her funny-bone.

The four horses crossed the ridge of Waxham dunes. Westerly breeze was cool where it blew along the coast. A freighter offshore, one or two people with dogs, emptiness for miles. Here on the beach there were no flies; the horses stopped swishing their tails and jerking their heads. Firm soft sand was inviting – what horse, what rider, wouldn't want to canter?

Here the farm land came to an end, joined almost flush against scalloped summer sea. No more wheatfields, woods, villages. No more rivers snaking through water-meadows past headless windmills, down cascades of watermills where decayed wheels hadn't turned for years, past rushy banks over which sails apparently without hulls dragged themselves across lowlands apparently without water. No more churches standing over fens where grebe and bittern breed, where marsh harriers tilt over reedbeds, where old vessels along dykes sink at their moorings. No more churches secluded in oaks and alders by their staithes. Here churches were gaunt fortresses against gales; they reared exposed from the last salt-bitten acres. Where the few copses that survived were stunted, every tree's back bowed, shoulders craven, arms hunched to protect cowed head, for parish after parish the flint church towers stood four-square, indomitably upright, guardians of the land, watchers of the sea.

Godawful flat charmless countryside, Emma Dobell thought. What was it doing, this lump sticking out into the least appealing of the world's seas? And the people who lived here, people like herself . . .

Shingle shelving under his horse's hooves, Benedict rode up alongside. He found it hard to bear when for minutes – sometimes it seemed for weeks – her mouth set so bitterly. In the old days it had been a singer's mouth. Its wideness had lifted, had smiled, had been sensual. Now its wideness just gave it greater possibilities for being sour.

"I'm glad Robert's coming to dinner," he said cheerfully.

"He's become dull." Her voice flat, featureless. "Why has he never done anything?"

"He farms at Durstead." Hurt jolted in his eyes (he had remembered Dick Clabburn smashed to death in a car); but Emma didn't look, didn't see it there. "What do you expect him to do?"

"Anything in the wide world. He could have waited till he was forty before he settled down to farm."

Her mouth reformed into its contemptuous line. She was too bored to discuss it.

"I think," Benedict defended his godson wearily, point-lessly, "I think he feels it's his duty."

She almost laughed, hadn't the vitality, drawled as usual instead, "Duty . . . ?"

How dangerous was it not to love the life one was offered to love? Fatal, probably, she thought; but there it was, she'd fallen out of love. Most people were so dog-like, she sneered, they'd adore anything – like this new brute of Benedict's that fawned on all the family, all except her, she'd noticed that. While for her – home wasn't home, it couldn't be if she didn't love it. Home was a countryside and a house she wouldn't miss . . . just as well, since she was leaving them now. Or was she equally dog-like? If the heart will give itself to whatever is presented . . . if there's no ugliness and stupidity we won't love rather than keep our hearts to ourselves . . . had she, who saw only vanity and void, fallen in love with them?

She clapped her heels into her horse's sides, forced it into the shallows. No, it couldn't be true. She hadn't fallen in love with anything, damnit, not even vanity and void. She wasn't capable of falling in love. Salt water is good for horses' legs, she thought; and then – Christ how often has that passed through my head over the years? why is the life of the mind so dull? yes, definitely it's a good idea to die.

That's right, convince yourself that what's going to hap-pen anyway will be a good thing, her mind mocked, that's what everyone does. "It's for your own good," she muttered to her sidling horse. "It's good for you." She laughed.

Benedict, hearing her, was glad she had cheered up; un-noticed, he too smiled.

Oh, but to die will be good, Emma dreamed, feeling sea water splash up from trampling hooves and wet her legs. Whatever lies or truths I can't distinguish between – could never believe in distinctions between . . . This, I think, will be good: to leave this home, leave this life I'm not at home in . . .

It's beautiful, look at those girls galloping along the sand, horses' manes and tails streaming, deer-hound careering after them. Yes, she was lucky, life had been so bloody picturesque. In the past she couldn't face it without senti-mentality, these days she couldn't face it without snickering. And if she couldn't produce healthier reactions than those, it was time to quit. Time to stop thinking of your daughters as girls too, she instructed herself, the elder will be thirty in a couple of years.

Good to be back, drummed galloping hooves in Alice's ears, oh good to be home. Neck and neck, the two horses swept along the beach. She glanced sidelong at Thérèse and smiled. Her sister's reserve seemed fractured by this rhythm, this speed, her shadowy face ignited. Knee to knee they thundered. Was that a stony patch? No . . . Soft sand could be dangerous too.

Alice felt wind tug through her flying hair. Wonderful to ride without a hat. Wonderful to have long hair – poor Thérèse never felt this delight, it just quivered close to her scalp. Life offered no finer moments than this, she realised she had forgotten Kit, cursed herself for remembering, forgot him again as her sister called, "Shall we jump this one?"

The beach was barred by wooden groynes built to control the longshore-drift; they made excellent fences when you knew there wasn't a quagmire on the landing side. "Yes!"

Alice cried, "this one's fine." She drove her horse at it, jumped, felt Thérèse jump beside her, glanced back and saw Zampa leap. On they flew. Panting of horses' lungs. Sand racing backward past head, ears, mane, shoulder. Drub of hooves. Creak of stirrup leathers. Singing of the wind that died away as they slackened pace, that died back into the hardly drifting breeze, the quiet of the faintly lapping sea, as they reined in, walked their horses peacefully.

"It's good to be back."

Thérèse cocked an eyebrow. "Even though you didn't want to be?" Her voice was kind, but dry.

Did Thérèse mean Kit throwing her over or Emma getting cancer? Alice's delight in riding vanished as if it had never been. It wasn't good to be back any more. They were discussing what didn't exist. She stared guiltily down the shore to where a furlong away their parents were hacking after them. Had Thérèse guessed how her faithless lover possessed her mind, how much of the time he excluded her dying mother? How mocking was this sympathy?

Blushing, Alice mumbled, "Oh, Milan was hell."

"Wearing fancy clothes, posing for photographers? Yes, it sounds dreary." Thérèse laughed non-committally. "Two or three of my stupidest friends always recruit their lovers from the modelling agencies."

"We can't all be brilliant young doctors," Alice said as good-humouredly as she knew how.

Though indeed after Cambridge she could have trained for pretty well any profession. Why had she never even wanted to? What was Thérèse saying, something about leaving France? She hoped that wouldn't mean she would sell the flat in the Marais; it could be very convenient.

"I'm sick of being overpaid for making the rich comfortable when they die."

So it was that the cardinal decision of Thérèse's life was explained to a sister thinking about herself too avidly to pay attention. Thérèse turned in her new direction very solitarily. Her fashionable Paris hospital did not yet know that among the specialists in this and specialists in that, one would leave soon to work for half her salary on relief missions where all hospitals were shacks and any equipment the medical teams needed they had to carry. In a graveyard on the North Sea, perhaps the ghost of Sam Mack standing among the yews smiled in benediction over her setting forth for tropics where he had gone before on the same errand. In a graveyard on the South China Sea, did the ghost of Gilles de Nérac pause in his strolling, smile to think his daughter was coming to look for him?

Alice wasn't listening. "Hell," Thérèse said, "I don't know. Probably I'm just running away from my inability to help Emma."

"What? Oh . . ." Alice was vague, conventional. "No . . . I'm sure it's not . . ."

Thérèse changed the subject to let her get her confessing done on the deserted shore.

"Coming back to Norfolk must remind you of Kit."

"Oh, yes!" What a darling Thérèse was . . .

How the morning sun fell on their clothes chucked on a wicker chair in a bedroom in Rome. The light fell in bars through shutter slats, shimmered on floorboards, iron bedstead, kicked-off shoes, a jug of flowers. How fine it was to wake on cool white smooth sheets, yourself being cool and golden and smooth. All that could be told. But how now it was impossible to get through the day because the morning sun to which she woke was always that Roman morning sun? How the more she tried not to think of it, the more she thought of it? And if she didn't try not to think of it, it was there, immovable, she couldn't get through it, couldn't go round . . .

Alice listened to what her voice was saying. It didn't sound like that at all. Something about insomnia . . . Thérèse saying brandy after dinner helped . . .

How getting through the year was such a fight – could that be told? Maybe she'd have a crack at years if she wasn't much good at explaining mornings.

How spring rain was the book she read that Easter in Touraine when it rained every day. The cottage roof began to leak, they crawled over the tiles trying to find the place. Then they had no dry firewood left, their clothes got sodden and wouldn't dry, spring rain was the cheap food they cooked, pigs' trotters, cabbages, it was the mould that grew on a pair of shoes, those soft mauves and greens, it was the mire in the yard, gutters spilling down. Spring rain was this, spring rain was that – how could she explain that it was never itself?

Alice glanced at Thérèse. She looked as if she was listening to something – maybe not something enormously interesting. That meant Alice must be saying something, but what?

"Zampa!"

That was Thérèse yelling. The deer-hound had mercy on an overfed woman walking an overfed Airedale, came bounding back.

Why was every moment hundreds of different moments? And why couldn't she control it? That was madness, wasn't it, not being able to stop one thought and start another?

After spring rain, damned summer rain. That was Kit saying, The way to walk through rain is very slowly with your shoulders straight and your head up. And he took her hand and made her walk slowly beside him – and it was a downpour – from one end of some Ligurian village to the other where the vineyards smelled of freshwater and the brooks sang.

"*La folie*," Thérèse murmured. That sounded about right, pretty appropriate comment, Alice must have been talking about what she thought she was talking about, things were looking up.

What about trying to explain how she was fool enough to believe Kit when he said he was still in love with her? That didn't make a lot of sense. Unless you understood how two people could get out of time with each other. Unless you remembered the sandbanks of Stiffkey years ago and how you had longed to be free and had broken your lover's heart as he now was free and breaking yours. Dancing out of step for ever they'd be . . .

All right, these dunes, tell how they're the dunes in Normandy – what was the place called? After dinner we walked along the shore, there were bathing huts – cosmopolitan Normandy, compared to Norfolk. We made love.

Thérèse will think that was pretty squalid. Let her. It was glorious.

I bet I'm crying, my words barge into each other, come out soaked and sibilant. The curve of that rivulet the horses are splashing through – that's the curve of the river at Sparta, the Eurotas that's right, we swam, the river was cold, there were pools and fallen trees, I saw a grass-snake swimming beside me, very beautiful, it's where Leda met the swan. And it's the curve of some wine I spilled on an oilcloth table. And the curve of a church window he's crazy about. How can I live through moments so alive with other moments? And the curve in an hotel wallpaper . . .

Thérèse walked her horse alongside Alice's, laid her hand on her shoulder. Did that mean Thérèse had understood? was bored with trying to understand? wanted quiet? Probably Thérèse thought the only thing that distinguished the liaison between Kit and her was the grandiose way it got talked about.

Cuckoo. Cuckoo. Mocking creature. That was at Fen House this morning, watching bees foraging in the lavender bushes. No, it was in that garden in the Appenines, Alice walked under the wistaria arbour, she smelled the wistaria, it was a soft evening. There was Kit, she saw him through the olive grove, he was watering the vegetable patch. The sun hadn't yet set but the moon was up, it was one of those moments when they're balanced either side of the sky. Cuckoo . . .

Why do I exaggerate? Alice asked each horse as she led them up the ramp into the horse-box. Feel better when I'm doing it, worse when I stop. This love of Kit's and mine will lose intensity in five years (*five years!*) or ten, who are we to escape the law of decay? Grimly she loaded saddles and bridles. Probably they'd just tell themselves their love endured . . .

She found the key in her jodhpur pocket. "I'll drive," she declared. Back into the muddy cab. Sun had beaten through the windscreen all afternoon, she started to sweat. All the shadowy women of Kit's imaginable escapades – did

Thérèse guess them? She must. Alice jammed the key into the ignition, turned it, the engine coughed, didn't catch, she sat without trying again. Did his conscience find his adventures innocent or reprehensible? Innocent of course. Did his sensuality find them exquisite or insipid? Some of each, no doubt. Which of their Roman friends? Which faces she had walked past?

The ponderous horse-box ground and rattled through shadowy lanes, through nettles and cow parsley, it rasped through overhanging alder boughs. Benedict was glad Robert Clabburn was coming to dinner. That common sense and good humour were just what were needed this summer – certainly were not to be dismissed as dull. He trusted the Dobells would not depress their equable guest too much. Emma gazed at a meadow they jolted by; she longed to be a child again who could lose herself in the enchantment of a shady wood-side, long grass, a weedy stream. Thérèse, travelling behind with the horses, leaned on the partition of the groom's cubbyhole. It had no window. She murmured to her charges – and she made a stern assessment. After three or four love affairs, and God only knew how many of the other kind, it would be vulgar to count, there wasn't a soul in London or Paris she would miss when she set off for the Far East.

━━━━◆◆◆━━━━

Alice lay back in her bath, gin and tonic balanced on the soap-dish. Steam wisped out of the open casement, sunlight and the smell of mown grass came in. Down a driftway through the wood, far off she saw dazzling green pasture. An irrigation hydrant fountained glittering arches of water pulse after pulse, swinging its jets around one way, then swinging back.

Would that bloody cuckoo never shut up? Didn't cuckoos knock off cuckooing at evening? Water sloshed, Alice writhed in her white iron coffin on its four wrought-iron feet, writhed as if a ghoul had become visible in the sunlit steam, had said, You've had your respite, now your torment will start again.

How goddamned long would this go on? Roughly she rubbed herself with a towel, roughly thrust her arms into her dressing-gown sleeves, roughly scooped up her riding clothes off the splashed floor. Any sensation was good. The stronger the better. Even pain. If this world would make more impression, maybe all the others would make less.

Her dresses twitched and flapped in the wardrobe, her hands brushed aside this one, that one. Something new, anything Kit wouldn't recognise . . .

Unfortunately the ordeal of the dressing-table was inescapable. Alice sat down to confront it. Pretty new pink dress, she snarled, well that's what hysterical blondes are for isn't it, wearing pink dresses on summer nights?

But her face . . . She leaned forward to the glass, despising herself for being absorbed, making no effort not to be. Beside her head, behind her across the room, on a chest-of-drawers stood the glass dome with its unchanging bee-eaters, golden orioles, hoopoes. But her face also changed too slowly to seem to change. These were the lines that betrayed her most cruelly, the lines of this forehead, this jaw, lines that were inexhaustibly rich in other moments, other scenes. The corners of her mouth, Kit kissing the corners of her mouth, they were rowing a skiff on Lago di Orta, but all the feckless wanderings of years were secreted in the modulation of skin where her lips joined her cheeks, this power of suggestion had no end.

No end? In panic she stared at her mouth, saw it part, heard her breath drawn in. Because like any human being she had a mouth. Because she had kissed and been kissed. In a skiff. On a lake. One day of innocence and cliché. Because of all this – would her mind go on ravelling *without end*? Was there no logical stop? Even when every cell in her mouth, in her brain had changed . . . No, wait! Only on Lago di Orta. Not on Lago di Como. Never. As it happened. The lines of her mouth couldn't suggest that. Oh, but they could! After the done, the thought of, then the not thought of, the only thought of now . . .

Alice jerked to her feet. She paced up and down till her breath was calm, till the tears in her eyes trickled back inside her head not outside. So this was what an obsession was . . . But they came to an end, obsessions, didn't they, yes, of course, they came to an end. What did sane people do to stop their thoughts ravelling? What were the deadeners? Drink, drugs, work, sex, God, lovingkindness – have mercy, not those last three.

Brush your hair.

Good. Without thinking, she sat down again at her dressing-table. She started brushing. That line her hair made, falling across her temple, Kit tracing that line with his finger-tips – but . . . something was wrong. She stared into the looking-glass. Unhappiness was the pleasure life offered, so she indulged in that. She raised her own fingers, traced the slanting line. What was it? Yes! She had changed her hair more than once since her lover ditched her. Pitiful stratagem: she had loathed herself for going to the most expensive place in Milan. The line had moved, he had run his touch an inch this way that evening they had strolled to look at which Roman church was it and then to a trattoria and . . . The new cutting and combing brought back the reason, changed the happy, loving Kit of Rome (no! already he must have been secretly depressed) into the Kit of Arezzo, miserable and un-kind. She heard him say, Alice, I'd rather be alone. Her last thought was extinguished, like the last civilised soldier to die fighting beside his emperor on the walls of Byzantium in 1453; barbarous hordes of self-pity swept into her mind, burning, pillaging, raping; she burst into tears.

Benedict Dobell, who had read Gibbon, who remembered the fall of Paris to barbarians in 1940, stopped on the landing. Like everybody else, in the war he had walked past women weeping. But he didn't want to do so still. Above all, not walk past his daughter, the chief good the peace had brought him. Nothing he could do or say of course. He dithered. But perhaps one didn't need to do or say anything. One could just be there.

115

"Alice."

He felt shy, going into her room. He thought of Emma and Thérèse making up their faces in their bedrooms. No, of course they couldn't have heard Alice weeping, they wouldn't come to comfort her. It was because it only took him five minutes to wash and change, on his way downstairs he had passed her door.

She sat hunched on a stool at her dressing-table, crying into her hands. He approached, she locked her arms round his waist, rammed her face into his jersey. He laid his hands on her quivering shoulders. She was brown where her collar dipped, in Italy she must have been sunbathing; how little he knew of her. Through the window, he saw a car bouncing along the drive. Robert had come.

The two men leaned on the paddock rail. Along the side of the covert, rabbits hopped about in the last of the sun, their white scuts bobbed.

"Do you fancy any of these horses?"

"You want to replace them?" Robert laughed. "Passing your broken-down nags on to me . . . I think I've got enough horses causing me enough trouble right now. But thank you for offering them."

They let the screaming of jets silence them, waited till quiet returned.

"Not replace them, no. That one I should get a few hundred quid for." Dobell pointed. "Those two I hope I can give to friends. That one should have been dead a long time, at the end of summer I'll ring up the vet."

"You've ridden all your life. You'll miss it."

Benedict thought, I shall miss Emma a lot more – or shan't I? He took out his case of cheroots, they strolled toward the water.

"I shan't want to ride alone."

116

"Come over to Durstead sometimes and ride with me."

"Thank you." The faintest of smiles. "I might do that."

Robert laughed his quiet laugh. "I quite often find myself exercising horses alone."

"Yes." His godfather regarded him. "I suppose you do." They strolled beneath an arbour uproarious with bees. "I wish I could keep horses for Thérèse and Alice, but . . . To feed and exercise them all year for daughters who come and ride half-a-dozen times . . ."

"You can't. But it's a shame."

And why did he keep horses at Durstead, Robert asked himself, horses to feed and exercise, horses he let his mother work hard to help him feed and exercise? He won races sometimes riding other people's horses, almost never riding his own. Couldn't afford champions. Couldn't strictly afford the decent point-to-pointers he had. Must just love horses. Could be a lot of fun even placing second or third in a steeplechase riding your own horse, a horse you'd trained, ridden every day.

Swallows swooped through the mild air, snapped up midges off the pond. In the shallows, frogs clambered on each other's backs. Iris flags flowered yellow. A moorhen and her chicks scuttled among the lily leaves. Dragonflies jigged, some diaphanous and blue, some diaphanous and green. Through the cooing of woodpigeons, a peacock raised its shriek, then a second, a third.

The grey head and the roan head dawdled on paths through rushes, from land waterlogged even in summer up to dry clipped grass. They had their rituals. Young trees to inspect. A sluice to discuss – should it be lowered or raised? Was it too rusted and rotten to lower or raise? Then there was a pair of woodcock to admire when they came roding over fen, two chestnut shadows wing to wing, grunting their throaty cry. In the orchard, there were bee hives to comment on. Godson knew the kind of conversation godfather enjoyed; he enjoyed it himself. He admired the mistletoe sprouting on one of the apple trees; noticed a walnut tree singed by a spring wind-frost; checked the mole-traps to see if any had been sprung. Under the lime trees they stopped

117

by silent consent to breathe the lime flower. Coming back toward the house, they praised the fruit forming on a fig tree by a garden wall.

"How's Alice?" Robert asked, having put the question off and put it off.

"Oh . . ." Benedict turned wearily from the fig tree. "Not very happy."

"He should have married her!" Robert blurted out.

"Do you think so . . . ? No . . . I doubt that would have done any good."

On the terrace, Emma Dobell tilted gin over the ice in the cocktail shaker, waved a vermouth bottle over it symbolically, crammed on the lid. Why was she such a fool? She had believed nothing could penetrate her numbness. She had believed that was her whole damned problem. The deadness of her spirit now. The living pain of dying of cancer later. People said it hurt like hell. Oh Christ oh Christ what a mess she was . . . And now, suddenly, coming out, seeing the walls of the house trellised with roses in flower . . . Very fine they looked, green stems and leaves, red and yellow and white flowers, climbing the white Regency walls. It would be roses, too. How banal! But she had minded that this was the last year she'd see the roses bloom. So now she was ashamed because it was the roses that grieved her, not her husband and children.

Dinner on the terrace was a ritual too, like the contemplation of sluices and trees. But not one Robert Clabburn could enjoy this evening. He had been shocked when he met Alice – she looked so plain. In any light less flattering than sunset, she would be ugly. What had Kit done to her? And how for that matter could she earn any money as a model? He guessed with different make-up . . .

She had felt his gaze. He blushed, raised his glass of white

118

Burgundy to her. "When I next see Kit, I'll kill him. But welcome home."

Alice raised her glass. It was one of a set of old Venetian glasses Kit Marsh had produced for some Christmas or birthday. Oh why couldn't we have drunk from other glasses tonight, the tired angel in her head mewed, is there no end to these stupid nicks of misery? Whimpering bitch, the resilient angel retorted, drink with Robert, smile at him too, he is kind, he hasn't changed, there are virtues in being home, you're lucky, be grateful, the tobacco plants smell sweet at dusk.

Mist formed in white swathes over damp meadow and lawns. A white barn-owl flew silently hunting over the grass. He disappeared behind a yew or an oak, came into sight again, searching for voles and shrews. Bats that had slept all day hanging by their heels behind drainpipes, in crevices under eaves, flittered their haywire flight. On the terrace, lanterns were lit. Even candles could be lit, the nightfall was so still.

After dinner, Emma sang. Oh, that's good, Thérèse thought, she's making an effort to cheer Benedict up, make it seem like twenty years ago, well done Emma, uncharacteristic but brave.

> Drink to me only with thine eyes,
>   And I will pledge with mine;
> Or leave a kiss but in the cup
>   And I'll not look for wine.

Thérèse glanced up, at her darkened window she saw her childish self in a white nightdress crept out of bed to listen. That was in summer. In winter if she had washed her hair she was allowed to come downstairs before bed and lie on the drawing-room hearthrug till her hair was dry, and Emma would be singing then sometimes while the wind made moaning noises in the chimney and you might hear an owl cry.

But what was she –? What the –? Oh no. Oh God no. That was the bloody trouble with drug addicts, you couldn't trust them for five minutes. What a goddamned song to choose to sing. When would she stop torturing that man?

> *Away, delights! go seek some other dwelling,*
> >   *For I must die.*
> *Farewell, false love! thy tongue is ever telling*
> >   *Lie after lie.*

Dobell's face showed nothing, he crossed his legs, tapped the ash from his cheroot. Alice dreamed of Italy.

She's half drunk, Thérèse thought, she's not thinking, or she's thinking sentimentally. What the hell, he married her, he must be used to it. How has she got so dishonest, so coarse? She wasn't born coarse. What stealing triteness . . . ?

> *For ever let me rest now from thy smarts;*
> >   *Alas, for pity go*
> >   *And fire their hearts*
> *That have been hard to thee! Mine was not so.*

This was unbearable. If this was the Old World, Thérèse would scrap it for the New any day, couldn't get to Cartagena quick enough. Where the Elizabethans had led, where Sam Mack had followed, she'd trail after. She picked up her glass of warmish wine, lit a cigarette, walked down the terrace steps, down the dewy lawn. If this was what was left of the lousy First World, give her the Second, the Third, organise a Fourth . . .

> *Never again deluding love shall know me,*
> >   *For I will die . . .*

Fine by me. Just don't talk about it. A pity – she'd always liked that song. All the fine things that got taken from you when you weren't expecting to lose them. When you hadn't guessed the next minute would be the minute to spoil something you'd held to your heart too thoughtlessly, the only way things can be held.

Why did Robert Clabburn have to pursue her?

"I'm sorry to dog you, but . . ."

"That's all right. What is it?"

"What *is* it? Why, Alice of course . . ." She waited for him to explain. "She looks dreadful."

"Yes, she does. Unhappiness can do that."

The grass where they strolled stretched away without glistening – there was no moon yet. Thérèse listened to Robert worrying about Alice; his voice spoiled the matt pond, the dim shapeless trees. Didn't he realise that no one was called on to marry an old sweetheart, it did no good? She told him. Didn't listen to his reply – presumably he protested.

"Isn't it splendid to hear Emma singing again?" Robert remarked, to steer the conversation onto a pleasanter course.

"You didn't listen to the words?"

"Oh, vaguely . . ."

Should she tell him how she despised her mother sometimes? No, that would be unkind. What about telling him that if Kit loved Alice till he died he wouldn't succeed in making her happy, Kit was far too solitary, he would never be happy loved by Alice either . . . No, Robert wouldn't want to hear that. It would interrupt his wondering how Kit had brought himself to be so unkind, how necessary and yet how difficult it was that Kit should be forgiven.

Metal clacked at the ground at their feet. A mole-trap had sprung. For a moment, Robert wanted to go down on hands and knees – anything to break this conversation he should never have begun – unearth the mangled velvet corpse, reset the trap. That was what Benedict would want done.

Flapping and squawking came from a tree; they had woken a roosting peacock. In the paddock, a horse heard the nightwalkers, trotted up to the rail.

"Look, Robert . . ." Thérèse had inherited her mother's drawl. "Why don't you go and be sweet to Alice?"

"Oh. Yes. All right."

Dismissed, he tramped away over the grass, leaving her alone.

At midnight, Benedict Dobell left his library and went upstairs. Going into his dressing-room, he stopped unnoticed in their bedroom doorway, breathing his wife's Gitanes.

Half undressed, half her make-up transferred onto a twist of cotton wool, Emma stared into the looking-glass. She leaned closer, raised her glass of brandy from the dressing-table, swigged, took a puff of her cigarette. She set the glass down, she swayed and giggled, she picked the glass up and drank again. Under her breath she sang,

Drink to me only with thine eyes . . .

III

Thérèse held her hands in the air, but her trousers and shirt were thin, some nettles stung her anyway. Still, the end of summer was killing them, they weren't as dense or vigorous as they had been.

"Just to your left," her stepfather said. "A chestnut I think."

She turned, waded through greenery. The white sleeve round the little chestnut tree gleamed.

"Found it."

"All right?"

"A bit overgrown."

The young tree had been suffocated by thicket, the sunlight it needed had been denied. Too late now for it to make any growth this year. But it had put on leaf, it was alive. And it stood upright, no gale had knocked it askew, unsettled its roots. Thérèse trampled down the nettles and thistles round it, tore the bindweed from its stem.

"And some more in that clearing."

Benedict Dobell pointed with the knobbed and gnarled blackthorn stick he wielded to beat through the tangle.

"I'll look."

"I should have done this back in May or June."

"I forgot too," she said.

She overlooked the fact that working in Paris she could

hardly be expected to tend Fen House trees. It was her way of telling him they were her trees too, she cared for them, alone in his Norfolk covert he was to sense her ghostly presence at his side.

A fallen poplar had made an ivy tod at eye level. Thérèse ducked. Plumage, chittering – what was it? Something bright flew away over the nettle-beds, was gone. Portugal laurels and hollies blocked her view, then opened out till she could see glade after glade. When the heads of trees stirred, sunlight shafting through the canopy swayed in the air like gauzy swags. Insects hummed. Alder cones fell in her hair, a cobweb clung to her sweaty face. Willow scrub tackled her legs; she staggered, barked her shin.

Thud. Thud. Farther off, Robert Clabburn and Alice were felling a tree. The wood encompassed them all – except her mother. But it was her mother dying that brought them together. No other year since her childhood had they all been at Fen House so often. Waiting . . .

Waiting meant keeping coming back. It meant giving less and less of her mind to Paris and to doctoring, the things she had desired, the life she had made. It meant repeated drives to the Channel ports or repeated flights to Amsterdam and Norwich, it meant a weary spiritless time. And a half-lived life in Norfolk when she got here – for hanging around the scenes of childhood, however dear those people and places might be, was like trying still to think with ideas she had grown out of years before. Well, it couldn't last. They sat around Emma's dying now, but when it wasn't there any more there'd be no point sitting round the gap where it had been.

Stay in Europe, Alice had said, stay in Europe for Bene-dict's sake. But no, no . . . She had to live for herself first, only then for others. Alice hadn't understood. There are aeroplanes, she had limply replied, sometimes I'll come.

Sometimes she'd come. But she wouldn't want to. Christ no. She loved Europe, but she didn't need to go on hugging it. That could get repetitive, the heart could go out of good things, she never wanted to do anything twice and already she'd started to.

And somehow Europe didn't seem much of a place any more. Or the Europe she happened to like was perishing. There were corners of a few of the ancient cities that were still dignified, that still had charm, where you could live amusingly. Where people still read books and still danced all night. There were adventures to be snatched still, if you aggressively made your luck, in lost stretches from the Baltic to the Aegean.

But too much countryside had been wrecked. There was North-East Norfolk that was home or had been, and was one of the fine places that still had a being of its own, one of the enclaves, served and blessed. And that wouldn't endure. Wouldn't outlast her mother many years. It was a spoiling continent. The style had gone with the power – trickled away through the first half of the century. Pity you couldn't have the former without the latter. Grace survived brilliantly after supremacy had passed – but only for a moment. Like when finally the music stops and the last dancers in silence but for the tapping of their feet dance the last dance better than all that went before. Then they put on their coats. Probably the other continents were spoiling too, for other reasons and in other ways. But she had not seen them yet.

Thérèse trod on one of Benedict's saplings. She stooped, straightened it. Why didn't he clear round his little trees? He always used to. This one had been smothered in under-growth, practically speaking its second year would be its first – if he remembered to clear round it next June. She knelt down, knocked back the scrub, adjusted the stake.

Her hands . . . stung, scratched, discoloured, nails broken and fouled. Hands she used to take such care of, beautiful hands she had been born with, slender and long, hands that deserved to be painted by Hillyarde for God's sake. Not any more. She was changing. She recalled recent interviews with international aid agencies; desks that dispatched doctors all over the globe; engines of salvation or of neocolonialism or both; help that Third World governments besought, tolerated, forbade . . . In a few years she'd know, know a little. Hands . . . She held them up to the sunlight ruefully.

Hands with which she could earn her living doing what she could tell herself was good. That was simple. That was one madness avoided with any luck, or postponed.

———— ◆◆◆◆ ————

Thud. Thud.

"Let me have a go," Alice said.

Robert Clabburn gave her the axe, sat down to rest on the first tree they had felled. When the wood was cumbersome with summer leaf, a gale had tilted two half-grown beeches into a third, all three had ended at forty-five degrees. Sawed up, carted, they'd replenish the wood-sheds, in a few months they'd be sere.

It was to fell these beeches he had driven over to Fen House. He had told himself they wouldn't get around to it without him – which was probably true. All summer he had kept coming over for one reason or another – even during harvest when he could ill spare the time, he who harvest after harvest had never left Durstead for a day till all his corn was cut.

Alice would recover, she must. Look at her now, swinging that axe as if she were cutting down the tree of treachery. White chips flew, the leaves on the tree being killed shuddered, leaves still sappy and green. Perhaps she had already begun to recover. Or perhaps she had not. Venomous, the way she handled that axe. And her face was still lumpy, her cheeks always looked like she'd been hit, her eyes and nose looked like she had a bad cold. Occasionally she had prettier days, when she had taken sleeping pills the night before.

When Alice was more tranquil, he wouldn't feel he had to keep driving over to be a distraction, be company. Emma would die. (All his childhood, she had been like a second and faintly exotic mother to Robert. He never knew how homespun she found him.) Thérèse would stop coming home, he wouldn't be bullied by that dry voice.

126

Alice would move to London and get some job or other. No doubt in time a new lover too. Already she made herself go down to London sometimes; but no job or flat seemed to get organised, she always came back.

A new lover. Or lovers. He didn't know which prospect repelled him more vilely. A love for which she might give up her freedom, or liaisons that wouldn't cramp it. Dear heaven, what a depressing choice.

Anyhow, his godfather and he would be left alone, fifteen miles and a generation apart as they had always been. Benedict with his daughters who showed up infrequently, with his library, with his deer-hound – nothing much else. He with his mother and his farm.

A jay flew by. Robert raised an imaginary shot-gun, swung . . . There was a gamekeeper in him. Jays are robbers of nests, there are too many of them, they need keeping down. He swung – but then he lowered his invisible twelve-bore. Ah let the damned thing go, Norfolk isn't a *paradiso* or a police state, let the marauder live too, he'd forgiven Kit . . . yes, he had forgiven him, he hadn't realised that before.

Sweat on the back of Alice's shirt. Stains under her armpits too. Thud. Thud. Thud. A beech takes a lot of felling. Hair sticking to her discoloured cheeks.

Now harvest was over, when autumn came there'd be less to do on the farm, he might fly to Rome for a few days. Talk to Kit. Find out if . . .

Sweat broke out under Robert's hair, coursed coldly down his face where the warm sweat of axing had just dried. What was it, he didn't know, his heart was a pile-driver, why the devil hadn't they carried two axes down to the wood, he could have got to work on that third beech, that was a tree of evil too. He stood up as a drunkard stands up when he's insulted in a bar.

"Robert, what's wrong?"

"Nothing."

She laid aside her axe, ducked her forehead, raised her sleeve, mopped.

"You don't look right."

"Nor do you."

"Oh shut up. I mean, I'm sorry. I know. I can't help it."

"It's my turn."

He picked up the axe.

"Look at my hands." She uncurled her fingers. They were blistering, so were her palms. "I haven't used an axe for so long."

"You won't get a job advertising soap."

"I wish . . . I wish I could just stay in Norfolk, cutting down trees, till I died."

"And planting them."

"In the winters, yes."

"Riding."

"Sailing."

"I . . . I think this tree's nearly down."

It creaked. Far off, they heard Benedict's and Thérèse's voices.

"You finish it. I'm tired."

"Yes. Of course." Why did he always fall into this stiff politeness? "Sit down and rest."

"I think I might go for a walk."

"Go for a walk?"

"Just for a few minutes. Here, in the wood."

Kit would understand, Robert was suddenly sure. Wasn't that a ridiculous thing to think? But Kit would understand . . . how he found himself on a fly-blown wasp-blown afternoon standing with an axe in his hand, Alice walking off through the trees in the opposite direction to the voices, smells of sap and crushed herbage in the front of his skull and nausea in the back.

When he had felled that tree, he felled the third. It took time, the axe was blunt now. Alice didn't come back.

Robert left the wood, walked over the rough grass to the yard, went into one of the sheds. No whetstone. Next shed. No. Third shed. He found it, spent five minutes sharpening the axe.

On the lawn by the ha-ha he found a congregation of Dobells and one de Nérac standing slightly apart smoking a cigarette.

"Don't worry about the vet," Alice was saying. "I'll see to all that."

"It's just . . ." Emma appealed to her husband. "We haven't used the boat all summer and I thought . . ."

"Take her rowing!" Alice begged. "Do . . . she'd love it, so would you."

"I'm sorry." Emma looked blank. "I always choose bad moments."

Robert said, "I'll go and catch up that horse."

Alice came with him. They fetched a leading-rein from the tack-room. In the paddock, the solitary survivor of the Dobell horses grazed. They ducked through the railings, walked over the cropped turf.

"*Come* along," Alice softly called. "*Come* along."

What's the noise we make, catching up a horse, Robert wondered, listening to Alice.

"*Come* along," she murmured. "Come *up*. Come *up*."

He looked sideways at her mouth, at how her lips moved. "Come *up*."

The old horse raised his head, stood still, let himself be caught. Alice clipped the leading-rein onto the halter. They started toward the gate.

——◆◆◆◆——

The path to the boathouse was overgrown. A decrepit Lord Derby apple tree had leaned and leaned until it propped one elbow on the boggy earth. Benedict went first, trampling through reeds. The sun clouded over, came out again. Vestiges of warmth glimmered, but summer was all but gone, afternoons passed quickly, grew cold.

Decoy, they called the place. In his father's time it had been a duck-decoy. The staithe was missing half its planks. A coot bobbed along the dyke with her nearly grown young in tow.

Zampa came lolloping through the reeds, scaring the

coots, almost knocking Emma down. Benedict unlatched the boathouse door, tugged it open against massed undergrowth. The jetty inside was slimy, the dog whimpered, refused to go on. She stood in the doorway, wagged her tail furiously to show how loyal she would have liked to be.

"Stay there, Zampa, I don't think we want you on board."

The boathouse was dank and dim. Fenders, rowlocks and bailers hung on nails on the walls. Oars were laid across beams; so were the spars and sails of a dinghy long sunk. This must be the first place I ever went afloat, Benedict thought. I expect Father helped Mother on board – was it this skiff? yes, probably – and then Nanny passed her the bundle that was me. He lifted down a pair of oars, got on board. A water-rat swam away. The hull rocked faintly, stirred the boathouse's first ripples that year.

The gates had not swung on their hinges since the war. They had been dragged open, tied back. Now skewed and greeny brown they mouldered year by year. Benedict wiped the thwarts with a sponge, handed the skiff out of the gloom into the sun where Emma stood on the staithe. Had anything except the gates' decay altered since 1920? Maybe the boathouse was in better repair then, the path cut. But the scene must have been pretty much like this. Only his parents' clothes had been a little different. But the modern age had introduced no telegraph poles here, no concrete, no plastic, no . . . Wrong, of course. He glanced up. Jets.

The boathouse dyke bowered with willows – then the small broad, weedy and still – then a narrow cut through the alder carr . . . And then the whole labyrinth, all the broads and rivers he and his brother had sailed to explore as boys in that pre-war world he could hardly conceive any longer when the rivers were clean enough to swim in, his brother who had been killed on a destroyer in the North Sea aged twenty-three.

He remembered how in summer they had loaded a sailing boat with sleeping-bags and a primus stove and set forth. How one night they had dropped anchor among reedbeds and shallows at Hickling and watched night fall on the ruffled stretch of broad, listened to wildfowl go to sleep in

the fen. Another night they had tied up along the river at
St Benet's Abbey, where in the ruins of archways the ruin
of a later windmill stands, where the grazed sward for acres
round is hard and lumpy with foundations, where swans
drift on the river, feed on the water-meadow. He remembered how half the farmhouses and barns round there have
bits of pre-Reformation stonework in their walls, how on
the river at dusk the air had been vibrant with mallard and
pochard, widgeon and teal, wisps of snipe came whirring
down.

Then in January, first the lily pond would freeze and you
could skate in a small way. Then if you were lucky and the
wind stayed in the north-east the broad which was deeper
would freeze too. He remembered his brother and himself
on winter evenings with hoses syphoning water onto the
thinly frozen broad, so that night the sheet of water on the
ice might freeze and in the morning it might bear; and
the gardener standing on the staithe saying,

Crack she bear, bend she break,
If you fall in you've made a mistake.

Creak and drip of the oars. Creak and drip, creak and
drip.

Half dead with her disease, the other half dead with the
treatment for it, in the stern Emma trailed her wrinkled
hand. Her rings glinted in the rippling light, a ribband of
weed clung. Between pain and painkillers, not much of her
was left to do any thinking. What was it Benedict had once
wanted to work out? She made herself try to focus. Whether
their water here at Fen House felt any reverberation of tides;
whether a thirty foot tide on the coast, when it had slopped
up rivers reach by reach, eel-set by eel-set, lifted their lilies
half an inch? Why had he wanted to know? Something to
do with whether it was private or not, whether the local
authorities would help pay for dredging. And what had the
answer been? Anyway the broad never got dredged, and it
was rare anyone came.

She felt her husband's eyes upon her, smiled her tired

smile. Some garganey were perched on posts that had once formed the cut out of the broad. Benedict's oar fouled on weed, he lifted it free. On the river, a pair of Canada geese swam.

"Which way do you want to go?"

"Oh . . . Just up and down."

He turned upstream. Like he did when he first rowed me here, she thought. She had recollected that, and had wanted to go rowing again before her last summer was gone. But now that flash of love for life had passed, she was back in her torpor, but torpor always uneasy because it might break unforeseeably, the pain of longing might flash in her mind, again fade away.

That year she came back from France with her little daughter, it had seemed so tranquil to ride along Norfolk lanes again and row on Norfolk streams. Then teaching the children to row, the sanctuary had been perfect still; the alder carr enclosed the broad in a green circle of peace. There was nothing else she wanted to do ever until she died. Mind and heart have to concentrate on this or that or some other thing; this was good enough, a good life to try to penetrate, try to live well. Then for days at a stretch she no longer thought of Gilles. And when she thought of him . . . To die in your thirties – that was an evil, for that neither Providence nor mankind should be forgiven. But . . . Quickly she had comprehended that her marriage with Benedict, lop-sided though it might come to be, would be pleasanter – at least for her, yes, she was selfish – than her marriage with Gilles would have become. Dancing at the blacked-out Ritz in London during the bombing raids . . . Dancing at the Ritz in Paris after the Germans had gone . . . Dying a generation later, she snorted with laughter, leaning on the gunwhale of the skiff. Gilles had been faithful for the first year after their wedding, not more.

Well, at least she had never betrayed Benedict with her body. Only with her soul, or whatever you call it. Not a lot you can do to forbid yourself that kind of treachery. If you are a self-betrayer, everyone who has dealings with you will naturally be betrayed, whether they realise it or not. The only thing is, you can make scrupulously sure the punishment visited on yourself is the worst – or anyhow tell yourself you're trying.

How could she make Benedict know how sorry she was? She couldn't. It was hardly likely now, after failing for so long. But she loved him now, if she loved him at all, because he had offered her the sanctuary he himself had not wanted because it should have been his brother's, but that he loved above all else. She had entered it because she had loved him – or had she loved the life they might lead? She looked at him now, a thin man with grey hair rowing a skiff that needed a coat of paint, keeping to the bank when a motorboat went by. The leather guards on the oars squeaked, he leaned overboard, splashed water on them so the squeaking stopped. Sometimes it seemed she could cram it all into a few sentences, all of how fine life had felt when she was in love too, before her soul or what-have-you had betrayed her as her body was betraying her now . . . Or had she killed her soul with vices of the soul, as she had killed her body?

Better not dwell on that. And she couldn't if she tried.

Better dwell on how they sawed up logs in the wood using that old two-man saw they called the long-man saw, taking a handle each and drawing the wavering blade to and fro across a bough; how with mallet and wedges they split the thick baulks; how then they loaded the billets into the saddle-bags on the tiny Dartmoor pony Thérèse rode, set off homeward through the glade.

That was the winter the pipes froze so the pump could lift no water from the well, Benedict lit a bonfire in the yard to try to thaw them underground but it didn't work, they had to melt buckets of snow on the stove. She bathed the children in heated snow-water in the tub they made bran-mash for the horses in, scrubbing them by the kitchen coal-fire.

Emma recalled going out each morning wearing Gilles' leather flying gloves, to break the ice that would have formed overnight on the horses' water-trough. How still it was at dawn, birds' tracks criss-crossing the white yard and the white field, snow yellow where a horse had staled. And then the dawn when she couldn't break the ice and had to fetch a pickaxe. How delighted Thérèse had been when she told her to get out her little sledge, they were going to haul it a mile to the village shop.

———◆◆◆———

"Benedict?"

He had seen her shiver, he was turning to scull back downstream. Her wasted body in her ancient tweed coat and skirt, her grey stricken face, filled him with dread, he still wasn't used to it.

"Yes?" he said, watching a skein of geese rise off a stubble field, come soughing overhead. Autumn had begun, there were more wildfowl moving in the sky every afternoon. A dozen mallard, two dozen, three dozen on the wing at once, high chevrons reconnoitring. "Are you cold?"

The last of the sun glanced through the alders. The broad was a pool of quiet, nothing but a few duck and moorhen moved. Then a fish reached for a fly, a sparrow-hawk crossed overhead. In the reedbed, the boathouse waited, rooftree sagging, staithe going down on its knees in weed . . . shadowy posts and slats where the skiff could wait till – maybe Thérèse or Alice would want to row one day next year.

"I don't think it's worth it," Emma Dobell said. "Going into Norwich for treatment."

Benedict rested on his oars.

Softly he said, "I think it's worth it."

"No . . . It's not." She smiled. "Sorry. Oh my love, I'm so sorry."

"It's all right. I understand."

"They can't cure me." The notion that, if only she truly wanted to be cured, there might be a one in a thousand chance, hung in the air, was dispelled. "The doctors, the equipment, money . . . they'd be better used on someone younger."

"I understand," he said again.

"No point in dragging it out."

Had he expected this? Kind of half consciously. So now it had come.

No dog to welcome them on the staithe. No horse in the paddock. Without thinking, Benedict walked over, closed the paddock gate. A hedgehog sensed him, stopped, curled up.

The evening trees cast gigantic shadows on the grass. The ha-ha was a black ditch curving across green. Was that a hare? yes, cantering off into the shrubs. Emma stopped halfway to the house.

"Benedict . . . Another thing."

Come away, come away, death, he heard in her voice.

"Yes, Emma?"

"If it gets too painful . . . If life gets so foul I can't bear it any more . . . Or I can see I soon won't be able to bear it . . . You won't mind, will you?"

"I . . . Yes. No."

"If I . . ."

He thought of the guns in the gun-room and felt sick. Or would she take pills or . . . ? Still, he'd do likewise. Not to die in the hands of others. And if possible not in agony.

"You'd be quite right."

"We'll talk about it."

"Yes. Tell me."

"Yes."

They went into the yard. The vet's truck had come and gone. Robert's car had gone. Thérèse and Alice and the dog must be indoors. A couple of peacocks and some fantails were pecking about.

Benedict noticed something hanging over a stable door. It was a halter. Carrying it into the tack-room, he saw it was blood-stained. He hung it up.

All these saddles and bridles . . . They'd have to be thoroughly cleaned one last time, then stored in the harness chest. But not now. He came out, shutting the door.

FOUR

I

Alice Clabburn laid her baby in the cot. Rose had not
wanted to go to sleep, she had cried and cried, Alice had
paced slowly to and fro in the darkened bedroom holding
her. She had murmured nonsense, any old nonsense so long
as it was soft and rhythmic and made a refrain. First Rose
had stopped crying, then just as Alice's back and arms were
beginning to ache Rose had shut her eyes and this time she
had not opened them again five seconds later. So a minute
after that, Alice broke the rhythm of her pacing, stopped
her murmuring, laid the baby down.

She stood still, listening. Yes, Rose was asleep. Why had
she been so difficult to get to sleep? Sensed her mother's
nervousness perhaps.

Alice went next door to her own bedroom to change.
Durstead Hall was one of those rambling Norfolk farmhouses built off and on over centuries in flint and red brick,
built with no particular shape or style, built with French
windows and Dutch gables but without a full complement
of either, built with no corridor straight, no two chimneys
alike, no room symmetrical, no two rooms on the same level,
no stair that didn't creak. Outside, there were no straight
lines either, and no clear divisions. It was hard to say where
the house stopped and the outhouses began. The garden
was mixed up with the vegetable garden, the stable yard

and the farm yard merged. Fields held their irregular shapes because of spinneys, tracks, ditches and boundaries long disappeared. Barns and cottages stood where they stood on account of agricultural techniques long obsolete. In one paddock lay a sheet of water at once horse pond, duck pond, lily pond. Lawns faded into meadows, shrubberies faded into thickets, then into woods, farm tracks became bridle paths and lanes became lokes.

From her window, Alice watched swallows swooping in and out of the broken window of the apple-loft where their young in their nests waited hungrily. It was a pity Rose was not yet old enough to be held up to see the swallow chicks with their gaping beaks. There came Robert, crossing the tennis court, coming back from his mother's cottage. His wife watched him pick up a twig off the lawn, then tread a bump flat, walk on. You needed local knowledge to win a game of tennis on that court.

Where was Robert going now? Oh, into the yard to see if Kit's car had come, he was looking forward to seeing Kit. And why was she standing so long at this window from which she could see the lane?

Clean skirt, clean shirt, take care not to think for more than your usual five seconds what to put on. Not very clean shoes, but who cares. And why shouldn't Kit come back to England? He was English wasn't he? He'd been away six or seven years, natural enough to come back. Or come home? She wondered which it was to Kit. Take care not to put on those earrings he gave you. Did he feel most at home working for a Roman faculty or a London museum?

Of course I want Kit to come, Robert had said in that voice of his with no ripple of irony. He had laughed his quiet laugh, a crinkling of crow's-feet, a puff of breath. Do you want to ring him up or shall I?

But when she saw Kit, would it all come back? Just thinking of him drawing closer through the lanes, what was it that was coming back in her? And if she couldn't stop it coming, how would she control it when it came?

Standing before her looking-glass, she tugged a brush through her hair. She was, she thought, more beautiful than when Kit had seen her last. The round cheeks she had as a girl had still been there at Cambridge, in France, in Italy; but they had gone, her face was deeper and finer now. She stood straight and still, turned sideways. No, having Rose had made no difference at all.

What the hell did she mean, *it*? There was no goddamned *it*. Her second and more tranquil love had suffused her mind with peace. Perhaps a peace less numinous than that brought by marsh tides long ago. Perhaps the coastal sky in her head was less radiant, its colours were softer. Oh but peace, innocent reliable peace in which Rose could grow up . . . No, no, you lying bitch, you were half enamoured of such peace before you dreamed of Rose.

For weeks she had known Robert Clabburn would ask her to marry him. He must have been pretty sure she would say Yes. Not wildly exciting. No. Shockingly sensible. Downright mature. If that many people are delighted when you announce your engagement, something is false. *Who ever loved that loved not at first sight?* Oh shut up. Lots of people. Yes, and what people, look at them.

Oh no, oh Christ, here it came, she had remembered a tail thin boy in Barton Turf church one Christmas Eve, how he didn't take communion, how he sat alone and gazed at the rood screen. All right. Remember that if you want to. But then remember how you gave him your heart and soul and he ditched you. Then try hard not to remember how at your wedding all your staid friends were so happy that you had recovered from your passion for that man who treated you so badly.

———◆———

All the way from London to Norwich, the country meant nothing to Kit Marsh. He had forgotten how far the commuter counties stretched, you had to drive two or three hours out of London in any direction before you came into true country, East Anglia was no exception. But north of Norwich he stopped fretting his ten-year-old Lancia was going to break down as it had on the way from Italy, stopped being irritated the English drove on the left so he couldn't see easily to overtake.

The true country was fine to be back in. It was a Constable evening, kestrels hovered over the fields, rabbits were nibbling along plantations. England seemed the greenest island in the world, good God what nonsense was this, well anyhow this was a pleasant green stretch of it. Though the chestnut forests of Italy were green, they were not green with the lushness of these straggly coverts of oak and ash, their shades of green were not so various, had not this softness. When he drove through Aylsham, the market was finished in the square. For some reason, the church bells were ringing, Aylsham had a peal of ten bells, they sounded clear and true in the bright air.

Turn right. Down a street of old houses, seventeenth-century beams and plaster, eighteenth-century red brick, then out into meadows and woods again, achingly familiar, time and again he had driven from Cambridge and later from the Courtauld to stay with the Clabburns. On these lanes, and on other lanes around Fen House, he had taught Alice to drive. On these fields Robert had taught him to ride. Well, they were Clabburns he was going to stay the weekend with now – just a slightly altered bunch.

Kit stopped his car, got out. Five minutes, just five minutes, he didn't want to arrive quite yet. He had chosen a bad place to stop. Ten years before, walking Clabburn lurchers, he had kissed Alice by this stile. Put that aside. Oh most severely put that aside. This landscape was . . . Well, what was it? Think, man. He was stiff from driving, he walked up and down to stretch his legs. He noticed cuckoo-spit on the long grass by the road, a cloud of gnats whirled in the evening sun. Get it straight: this landscape was love for Alice, but it wasn't home. No more than Rome or London were home. Likeable places – but he didn't have a home in the Clabburn or Dobell sense, what had all that crap about green English woodland meant, he should

142

be ashamed. Italy for a few years, England for a few years, got to be somewhere; but let's have no wishing you were otherwise, no longing to be home, there is no home.

He forced himself to see himself come out of a theatre with Alice. They crossed Shaftesbury Avenue, went into a little Chinese place, sat down to eat. There he had said, Alice I'm going to work in Rome, will you come with me? And she had said Yes, Kit, yes I will. That had been a betrayal, though he hadn't known it at the time. But ignorance was no excuse – not for a second could he believe it was. He had betrayed Alice then; at the moment of loving her most he had betrayed her most. It led straight to Arezzo. Get this clear in your head damn you before you drive on. I've had it clear in my head for years. Yes, but think about it very plainly once again. To Arezzo, it led. Remember her that rainy night, her dark blue cape, her beret on her bright hair, how she said Go if you're going, I'm all right, goodbye my love, and he walked away by the grey majestic houses and turned once and she was still standing where the streetlamp shone on the wet paving and a torn poster flapped on a wall.

Are you sure you comprehend how solitary you are? Sure you want to be as solitary as you think you want to be? Dead certain? There won't be any weakening as years go by and increasingly life seems a balls-up? No unnecessary melancholy? No, certainly not, just the reasonable, the correct amount. No going back on decisions of that magnitude, that would be to have betrayed too frivolously, wasted too generously, that would be suicide time all right. You're either alone in this world or you're not. Right? Right. Then get back in the car. Drive through Robert's land. And never envy him his house, his peace, his wife, his child. Oh God the child. He'd forgotten the child. That wasn't going to be easy. He recalled the time Alice had an abortion. Steady, enough of that. What had they called her? Rose, that was right. Pretty name. Better than all the biblical names people gave their children. Rosa Mundi. Don't be silly. The Rosenberg. Cima Rosa. For pity's sake.

"Where is Rose?"

They were in the hall. It still smelled of French polish and sounded of dogs, no change to the chests and vases, much the same flowers.

"In bed asleep," Alice said.

"Can I see her?"

"Yes, of course you can. Oh Kit it's good to see you."

He grinned at her as he hadn't grinned for years, felt laughter rise to his lips, a laughter of delight he could not remember the sound of any longer. "It's damned wonderful to see you." It had been odd in the yard, the way she deliberately fumbled their embrace, made nothing of it. As soon as she touched him he had understood, he had done likewise, cursed her for communicating so faultlessly with no words spoken, with no eyes meeting even, just with touch.

Kit asked, "Where's Robert?" Why was it Robert he suddenly wanted to see most of all? Was he so attractive because as Alice's husband he possessed Kit's dominant love? Because so long as Alice was Robert's, Kit was free? Simply because he had loved him for so many years?

"Right here," Robert Clabburn said, coming into the hall. "I've just been down to see my mother."

And then, thought Alice, you found some chore in the stables so I might have Kit a first minute to myself.

Robert hesitated in the doorway. So there Kit stood at last. Oh good, good.

Kit started striding to him over the flagstones. Alice watched his crumpled linen suit move away, his lank shape, his gangling arms and legs. Still Robert didn't move, she had never seen him shy in his own house before, slight with his jockey's slightness, tense, poised but poised nervously off-balance. She saw him hold out his hand, saw Kit take it, then heard Kit say I'm feeling Italian and grip his arms round Robert's shoulders. She saw Robert grin with pleasure, saw too he didn't know how to feel Italian, saw how awkwardly he embraced Kit. The one with muscles of whipcord. The other always unfit, he would live for weeks on coffee and oysters and wine.

144

"I'm going to take him up to see Rose," Alice said. "And show him his bedroom."

"I'll get us all a drink," Robert said. "I put some champagne in the fridge." He hesitated again, still gripping Kit's elbow. "Can't tell you how glad I am you're here."

"It's been too long."

"Dead right it has."

"Silly." No, Kit thought, that's the wrong thing to say. "I mean, it just happened, I haven't been in England."

"I thought of coming to see you once. Years ago."

"Idiot. You should have come."

"You never came to see me."

"Well, er, no . . ." Kit blushed. "I . . ."

"I'll get that champagne."

Upstairs, the landing creaked.

"Robert said you often stayed in this room."

"That's right, I did."

He set down his suitcase, they went on along the landing, Alice walking softly ahead. Kit tried to tiptoe after her so as not to wake Rose; he found the effort made him tremble, or he was trembling anyhow. Robert had been shaking too. What fools they were! He watched Alice walking ahead. That obscure object of desire . . .

"This is her room."

Kit stopped. He heard a faint breath of laughter beside him. Alice had picked up her husband's laugh. Then he felt her hand lightly on his back, urging him into the dim bedroom.

He bent over the cot, but he couldn't see much. Alice leaned beside him and straightened the bedclothes. Engagement ring, wedding ring . . .

On the staircase again, Kit said, "I couldn't really see her face, but I'm sure she's beautiful."

Alice stopped, turned to him, said nothing but looked very steadily into his eyes. Not cold, not flirtatious, just steady. Honest and loving and sad. Her eyelashes never moved, the grey flecks in her blue eyes neither darkened nor lit up. A floorboard creaked. A moth fluttered at a pane.

Just as he felt he could hold her gaze no longer without tears, she went on down the stair.

So Kit had his answer. Alice had been worth loving all those years. He had not been mistaken in her. She could have appeared the happy young wife, could have prattled about the baby's features, health, habits, God help us even her clothes. No doubt often Alice was a happy young wife. But she had the honour not to retreat into that, not to act it to him.

In the dining-room that steady look of hers was still with him. Why did it seem familiar? The Bellini of course, he had forgotten but yes, that Magdalen had that calm wide gaze. Time to go back to Venice, look into those eyes again. No, why bother? He could bring them to mind perfectly, he didn't even need to glance at Alice to know that lustre of skin and fall of hair he had idealised for so long.

So . . . With that slow look in her eyes, with that courage, Alice would not play things up nor play things down. She would not play at all. Would try to ignore nothing, conceal nothing. But how could Robert and he live up to such honesty?

The thing that made life all right was that Alice and he could never betray Robert. Couldn't want to. No, wrong. Would want to; but far more powerfully would want not to. Could hardly conceive of it. He just had conceived of it. Horribly attractive she had looked, walking before him along the landing. Conceived of it – but conceived of its impossibility. All right.

––––––◆––––––

Robert Clabburn gazed out of the French window at flower beds becoming dim in the dusk, the sky going violet, massed leafage of the trees merging into each other and into gloom. Then it was good to turn back to the oval mahogany table, to the fireplace with no fire, to Kit Marsh who had

146

been an attendant daemon of his marriage, whom it was so fine to have here where he could be seen to be a good daemon, affectionate and kind.

He had been pretty confident Kit would not mind him marrying Alice. Don't worry about him, she had said. He doesn't want me. He'll be pleased to think you have a use for me, find me amusing. But all the same Robert was contented to meet Kit's smile and know he was happy to be here with them. If only seeing Alice again didn't make the poor devil too wretched thinking of all he had given away.

Of course Kit was still in love with her. There are people who fall out of love, and there are people who do not fall out of love or who tell themselves they don't. Only a fool would marry one of the former. He, Robert, had married one of the latter – and that might have been a mistake too.

She lived in her love for Kit Marsh like one lives in a climate, could no more stop it than she could stop the rain. She lived in her love for her husband as inescapably as that too – but it was a more temperate climate. Hell, let's hope they can love each other temperately too, Robert brooded, they'd better, if not we're done for, all three.

"You didn't come to our wedding," Alice was saying.

"I was in Greece. I thought it might seem a bit exaggerated to come all that way."

"It would have been wonderfully exaggerated."

"Did Thérèse come?"

"Thérèse came from Mozambique."

How could Kit tell them how he had sat in the courtyard of that house on Zakinthos, the house where he was staying with a lover, sat by the white-washed well under a datura they also call angel's trumpets because of the shape of their flowers? How he had imagined a marquee on the lawn at Fen House and Benedict Dobell's smile and then had remembered datura was supposed to give you strange dreams. How he had stood up because he was too restless to sit still and had paced back and forth in the courtyard from the angel's trumpet to the orange tree, angel's trumpet, orange tree, back and forth till in England the wedding must have been over.

"Which lawn did you have the marquee on?"

"The lawn below the terrace."

Yes, he'd imagined it right. He could never tell her how he had imagined everything second by second, imagined it for a long time before and then during and then for a long time after – but probably even through her excitement that day she for a moment imagined him imagining it. One day he might tell Robert and her the stupid story of how he had expected to get a headache. His head had an excellent repertoire of aches suitable for most eventualities. He had been sure a new ache would be forthcoming on this unprecedented occasion, an interesting new pain or a familiar pain shifted to a new part of his head. He had waited. The hour of the wedding had struck (he had ascertained the time difference between England and Greece). No headache. Extraordinary. And then, for the first time in his life, his nose had poured with blood. He had lain on his back in the courtyard. He had thought of the wedding guests getting into their cars and driving away; he had wandered into the marquee empty after the party and breathed the trodden grass; he had come out into the sun again and found Benedict and Thérèse left talking on the terrace while caterers started clearing up all around. Then the Italian lover had come into the Zakinthos courtyard and asked why he was lying on the ground.

"I missed you," Alice said. "You know, secretly Robert wanted you to be his best man."

Kit's eyebrows arched in a manner they had not known how to do before he lived in Italy. "You didn't get married in church did you?"

"Good God no." Alice smiled at her husband. "Though Robert wouldn't have minded. But you can't marry a faithless slut like me in a church."

"I didn't care either way about the church," Robert said. "But I would have liked you to be there."

"You didn't even send a telegram."

"I did." This was a story he could tell. "Three villages

away there was a post office. I walked. It was hot, but it was a pleasant walk over the hills through the olive groves. I sent the telegram, walked back in the evening. It grew cool, there was a breeze off the sea. A week after your wedding, a message came for me, would I go back to the post office. They had been unable to deliver the telegram because the address could not be understood. I checked, some Greek telegraphist had scrambled it hopelessly. I don't think the Roman alphabet meant a lot in that village."

"What a sad story," Robert said.

"I was angry at the time. But quite soon I thought it was funny. You see, I had been trying to think I was a Chekhov character, trying not to take myself seriously. So when this happened, exactly as if I were in a Chekhov play, I thought, that's marvellous, what the hell, I don't have to try, I *am* like that, these things happen to me."

Robert said, "We missed Emma too."

That unforgivable way the married say "we", Kit thought.

"If Emma had been there," her daughter declared, "she would have been a ghost." Alice was still haunted by how contemptuous her mother might have been. She had not ended a great believer in second loves. They might be the most agreeable issue under the circumstances; but that wasn't saying much if you had any pride. Alice woke sometimes in the night hearing that drawl: Marry Robert, darling – what for? "She did right to kill herself."

Kit swallowed. "I didn't know . . ."

"Yes. In her car."

After dinner, Robert asked, "Is he worthy to see our barn-owls?"

"Oh . . ." She pretended to consider. "I should say so. I'll go and change."

"You dress specially for your owls?"

"They like women in jodhpurs."

They walked out to the paddock, Robert carrying a bottle of Calvados and three glasses which he balanced on the rail.

"I'll catch you up a horse, Kit."

"Do I need a horse?"

"Owl-watching is best done on a horse."

"So is Calvados-drinking," Alice elaborated.

"The owls nest in the stable loft. Over there. Look. That's the window they use. We noticed them feeding their young. Last night we saw the owlets come out to learn to fly."

"They think we're part of our horses," Alice explained. "At least, they don't appear disturbed however close we come. Or they think we're centaurs."

Damn you if you covet this life. Even for a moment. Even silently. Damn you to hell. But Kit thought of the poky flat which was all he could afford. A career that could perfectly well have been pursued by someone else, love affairs that could have been anyone's, life lived on Jameson and Camels. Come on, it isn't that bad, a ballet next week, oh terrific, sometimes I live a month on Ricard and Gitanes instead, life is various. Some months I live on food too, there's always Martell and Sullivans, if I have to go to another dinner party I'll commit suicide, if I have to cook another solitary omelette I'll commit suicide, life is sweet.

◆━━━◆━━━◆

Robert clipped a leading-rein onto a head-collar, gave Kit a leg up, handed him the end of the rein. The horse broke into a trot. Kit had not ridden bare-back for years; he jiggled uncomfortably, his legs didn't grip. Thank God Robert had given him a placid creature to ride. There stood the stable. But he could see no owls in flight. Which section of rail bore the Calvados? Gingerly he urged his mount that way.

Then Alice was here, she was beside him, sitting her horse with her long legs dangling – the old magic got him by the brain and shook. You would not be starting to regret Arezzo, would you? Arezzo was the one incontrovertibly honest action of your slipshod life, damn you, remember that, don't whinge. Didn't you swear years ago never to pray and never to whinge? Stick to that. Missing her is just missing her, it has no importance. But never to hold her in your arms again . . . That is only selfishness, give it no weight.

It must be the effect of the green woods by day, of the canopy of stars by night. Was Britain a green island if one had seen Sri Lanka and Borneo? Probably not. He must remember to ask Thérèse. If he ever met her again.

But to have Alice and to hold her . . . Ah come off it, you weren't happy when you had her. Yes, but that may be something to do with not being happy, nothing to do with Alice.

Those legs of hers. The slimy jerks who hang around mannequins and how jealous you were sometimes. That so grand and oh so chic connoisseur, he had a gallery, a man of the highest education, a man of refinement, I am sure you understand, who offered you a job but it wasn't you he was after. Hell, it wasn't that bad – we amused ourselves annihilating each other's admirers – it was part of the game – be honest, you enjoyed it.

Remember Rome before you knew that what you would long for above all would be to be free. Yeah, well, before you realised how necessary that disgraceful thing solitude is. When neither you nor Alice did much thinking – but it was wonderful to cross the river in the morning light, go into Campo de' Fiori to drink cappuccini and eat brioches. How then you strolled through the stalls with their awnings, her hand in your elbow, her straw hat tilting shade across her face. Great stuff – do you fancy the stylish effusion on the subject of her freckles now, or should you hang onto that for later? Later maybe. Good freckles, though – the way in the spring in Italy they appeared on her cheekbones. How we bought fruit and salad, fresh bread that smelled good, a bag of roasted coffee beans and a bunch of flowers with their good smells.

"You're far away," she said. "Where are you?"

"I'm in Rome."

His horse sidled, stood still. He let it lower its head to crop the grass.

"I was in Rome too." They talked softly on account of the owls and because on a still night it seemed the natural way to talk. But Rome whispered was more dangerous than Rome spoken would have been. "I was in the gardens at the Doria Pamphili . . . I often am . . . walking under the trees with you."

Here came Robert, Kit heard the soft thump of his horse's hooves, heard him say, "No owls yet," quietly. Then, "I've brought the bottle. Do you want some more Calvados?" Here too came joy, suddenly it filled the grassy night, this was a new beginning, Kit understood, Robert and Alice must understand too . . .

Kit heard his voice murmur, "Calvados will never taste so good again." He heard his heart cry to Robert, Can this be a new beginning, please can it, I think it can. There is a languorous delight in wanting your love to be successful and happy; there is a languorous delight in wanting my love to go on being the failure it is. I love your marriage as fervently as you love it. More fervently perhaps, but we'll overlook these charming small perversities. I so passionately wish you well – let me wish, let me love, and all, all will be victory.

Of course, his love for Alice had come back. Or it had never gone away. Sometimes it had seemed to go away. Sometimes in the early phases of a new affair his love for Alice seemed to go away as if it didn't reckon on coming back. But the new lovers always became old lovers, then were half forgotten. And Alice had never gone away, not far away. She just hurt less when life was amusing, hurt more when life was melancholy and he drank too much. There was a rhythm to his missing her, that was all it was, there were squalls and there were lulls.

But to value Robert's love for Alice higher than his – to be a loyal servant of their happiness . . . This would be a good use for a heart too often indulgent and lazy. This would be a love to work away at decently over the years. It wouldn't be too bad. Bare-back on a thoroughbred by the North Sea, louche days in Rome seemed very far away. But the fine feeling of not regretting Arezzo was here, was now, was inspiriting.

"Owls," Robert Clabburn whispered.

They watched them glide along the wood. Sound of horses' teeth ripping turf. Ghostliness when the flapping shadows crossed the meadow, crossed open starry sky.

It was there, Alice Clabburn could feel it, her love for Kit was there where it had always been. Usually she contrived to ignore it. Since that love could never be happy, it had seemed fittest that it should be ignored – and when it could not be ignored it should be savaged. She had done a fair amount of savaging of her love. Then when she and Robert had come to love one another in their gentle way, she had married him to put paid to her wilder love for ever – and because, if she were to marry anyone, Kit's beloved Robert was the husband who would hurt Kit least.

But it was still there after all the pathetic ignoring. When she woke each morning, her love for Kit resumed its place in the world along with her bedroom ceiling. It was utterly simple, as Wittgenstein said of the *a priori* order of possibilities that is invisible but runs through all experience, as it seems from before the beginning . . . without cloudiness, without uncertainty, purest crystal, everywhere . . .

The savaging hadn't done it any harm – had been a sorry gesture to propriety, no more. Despicably conventional to abuse her old love, pretend it had not been as glorious as she knew and Kit knew it had been. The savaging had been cowardly and a waste of spirit. Her passion wasn't that paltry, it shrugged off insults, set its teeth and endured railery, it was made of resilient stuff alas.

"I think we've seen our owls for tonight." Robert swung his right leg over his horse's withers, slid down to the ground. "They're back in the loft."

Jesus Christ, hadn't these two learned *anything* in the last five years? He had heard them talk – this and that – someone they had met at the Pantheon, who walked a lion cub instead of a dog – sounded crazy, didn't it? Oh voices, it doesn't matter what you say, your voice will answer for you, you're betrayed . . .

Maybe there was something to be said for old-fashioned love affairs that came to grief when one or other of the lovers fell out of love. A bit of mutability, that was what was needed, a bit of transience for God's sake. Kit was mad, Alice had been bloody right about him, he never fell out of love, just decided he didn't want the affair. Saw no reason why love, just because it existed, should be satisfied. No indeed. Most rational. Didn't think indulging in this selfish emotion necessarily led to any virtues, or even to much amusement. So sane Robert could kill him. No, that wouldn't be rational, would it? More coherent that he should kill himself. What was it that madwoman Thérèse once said? All love affairs are unsuccessful, they either end in nothing or in marriage. The kind of bullshit she'd call a joke. Well, this love affair in his house now appeared to be an exception.

Going to bed, Robert stopped on the landing, went into Rose's room. Alice had picked her baby up. She sat on a chair by the cot, feeding her at her breast. He heard the mild sucking sound, smelled the sweet skin smell of his daughter that always made him want to hold her face to his face. Alice looked lovely in the dimness with her shirt unbuttoned, her head bowed, bright hair falling forward. When her husband came in, she smiled.

To get it over with, he asked, "Why don't you have an affair with Kit?"

"What," she laughed, "another one?" But then she pulled herself together. Her candour came back. Her smile dilly-dallied, but went at last. "Oh . . ." she breathed, "if only we could . . ."

This honesty will be the death of us, Robert thought. His voice asked, "But you can't?" Her voice answered, he tried to pay attention, to remember, but depression had filled his skull with pig-iron, his chin kept sagging down to touch his shirt. No she couldn't because she was his wife – "I love you and I am yours," he focused on that bit. And something about Kit loving him too much too, did he believe that, yes, probably, but it wasn't the point.

When I married her, I knew she would have married Kit if he had ever asked her, what's wrong with me now?

"No one except you will ever know about my love for Kit," Alice said. Oh marvellous . . . What was she murmuring now? He must have asked a question. "Oh hell, I don't know, Robert. My love and Kit's love . . . Why try to satisfy it? It can't be satisfied."

He must have asked her if she wanted to go away, because he heard her say, "No, Robert. I hope you might wait for me. This will pass, dear heaven it has to pass. I hope you might forgive me."

Then he was gazing at that sleepy feeding armful there, thinking, I might as well get divorced before I get more devoted still. Wait, forgive, yes, well, I'll try, have to for Rose's sake don't I?

When he had gone, Alice sat for a long time. Rose fell asleep in her arms.

II

Horses.

Horse-boxes waiting empty. Horses sweaty from the last race, a hurdle race, being led down the line of loose-boxes. Horses whinnying. Acrid smell of straw where a horse had staled. Grooms coming and going with tack. Horses being saddled up for the next race, a steeplechase, the Queen's Cup, in which Robert would ride, though not a horse of his own.

Grey Easter Monday sky, North Sea wind moaning over Fakenham Heath, over parked cars and marquees and race course, over far leafless hedges, far growing wheat. Wind juddering Kit's hair and swirling Alice's when they left Rainbow in the loose-box waiting for the last race, left the boy to look after him, tramped quickly through the gale.

"You'd think it was going to snow."

"It might. I've seen Robert ride in snow."

Horses being led into the paddock and walked round by their stable boys. The runners for the next race up on a board that looked like a guillotine. Number five, Lullaby, Mr R. J. Clabburn. One of the only two amateurs riding. Bookies on their stands in a rank, semaphoring signs Kit couldn't decode. A thinning crowd round the Tote, a thickening crowd at the paddock rail.

The best place to watch was out on the course, Alice liked

156

to stand by an open ditch, you found hardly anyone there, it was the finest way to watch horses jump. But when Robert was riding she never had time. The paddock to see him mount. The members' enclosure to watch the race. You could never see very well, but she hated the grandstand, she felt trapped there and cut off from Robert. Then the winners' unsaddling enclosure if you were in luck, then always loose-boxes and cars, occasionally the ambulance.

The sky had never been lower. Murk whipped past Kit's watering eyes. But he was baled in wool and tweed, so was Alice, how cold would Robert feel in thin breeches and colours? Kit hoiked his race-card out of his pocket. There was Robert again; and Lullaby, owned by somebody, trained by somebody, placed third last time out, not placed the time before, second before that, not the favourite Alice had said but fancied. He heard snatches blown from the loudspeaker, Number five, ridden by Mr . . .

Alice kept being stopped, spoken to. Sometimes she introduced him to people. Kit Marsh found he instinctively liked them all, they meant Robert and Alice had accepted him, understood how passionately he wished them well; he could keep visiting Norfolk sometimes, all was going to be well. So he shook hands, he smiled, he talked; these were all faces he would be cheerful to see again.

Old Mrs Clabburn he knew. But who was this white-haired man with a stick beside her, with rheumy eyes, with blotchy skin? His tweed suit and tweed overcoat had been well-cut a generation ago. His shirt had been made for him too, though now the collar was frayed around his scrawny throat. Mrs Clabburn walked slowly so the stooping man could keep up.

"Kit, you remember my father."

And how could he suddenly say, You're the one man to whom I'd like to explain that I may not be the shit you think I am?

"I'm very g-g-glad to see you again." Kit's stutter came back after ten years. The crowd elbowed them on all sides, they shook hands but it didn't really work. "C-c-come and t-t-take my place by the rail."

"Thank you. I was delighted when Alice told me you were back in England. No, no, please keep your place. I know Robert can get on a horse."

Kissing her father, Alice Clabburn knew more than ever that she must get rid of Kit, this friendship wouldn't work, she knew Benedict had seen her bright eyes, this wasn't any race meeting. This wasn't Fakenham at Easter Monday last year. It wasn't Fakenham at Easter Monday in the late forties when her father and her dead father-in-law rode this race, it was called the King's Cup then, and one of them won and the other was second, she'd forgotten which, anyhow it hadn't only been once.

Only his mother watched Robert Clabburn walk into the paddock with the other jockeys, saw him talk to Lullaby's trainer, saw him not show how cold he was, saw him mount and ride onto the course. She knew Benedict was only there, feeling old and ill, because his godson was pleased when he came; he stood slightly apart from the crowd at the rail, and couldn't see. She was certain Kit and Alice hardly saw when they looked; knew this was Kit's doing and loathed him for it; despised Alice for being so moved. Her daughter-in-law had not always been so coarse. When she married Robert, Mrs Clabburn had ceded first place in his affections delightedly. She had loved Alice's ill-concealed pride when he rode, loved her nervousness. But those days were gone.

In the enclosure, Kit Marsh talked politely to Mrs Clabburn; he wanted to leave Benedict to Alice, though he hoped one day he might speak to him alone. Mrs Clabburn had been kind when he was a boy; ever since then, he had felt uncomfortable that he found her priggish and dull. He got a break from his politeness when the field came past the post first time round, still bunched up, Lullaby going steadily in third place, Robert's roan hair hidden under his jockey's cap. Then there were just his white breeches among other white breeches going away, they jumped an open ditch, then a left-handed turn downhill to the water-jump and they went out of sight, nothing but wide green and wide grey, loudspeaker talking, then lost dots of brightness on the far side of the course. He's catching them, Kit heard

Alice cry, Benedict he's catching them, look Kit, oh look. And Kit looked and saw nothing, then the race came out of the hollow with two fences to jump, he tried to pick out Lullaby's colours, he'd forgotten or they all looked a brilliant blur. He couldn't hear Alice for the shouting all around, beside him he noticed Benedict could see nothing, would wait on the event. They were jumping the last and was that Lullaby, was that Robert, Lullaby landed and galloped clear, and here he came though you couldn't hear the hooves for cheering, here he came.

Alice didn't know whom to hug. She knew she was a fool when Robert won, always would be probably, just for an instant she could never believe how wonderful he was. Then she realised she didn't want to hug anyone. So she simply stood, feeling golden. In a minute she would remember how to be modest – not yet.

Kit had no cognisance of the next race. Mrs Clabburn and Benedict Dobell being quiet about Robert's success. Alice fussing over Rainbow who was entered for the Prince of Wales' Cup later. Kit himself aware he was talking too much, aware he didn't know how to help.

Race-card again, loudspeaker and guillotine again: Rainbow, owned and trained by Mrs R. J. Clabburn, ridden by Mr R. J. Clabburn. Night would fall before long – if it didn't snow first. How did Jack Yeats paint these scenes, maybe Ireland isn't as cold as East Anglia, don't they get the North Atlantic drift, no man would set up an easel in this wind. Bookies still trading with stentorian jabber and mittened gestures. Horse-boxes leaving with horses that had already raced. Some cars leaving too, not waiting for the last race.

Alice was afraid her entourage would want to come into the paddock. Robert disliked a bunch of hangers-on. But she should have known – her father kept Kit and even Mrs Clabburn out of the light.

Among the knots of owners and trainers in the paddock, Alice stood alone. Thoughtfully she watched the boy lead Rainbow round. She watched her own initials on the horse-blanket go by. The horse looked all right, he wasn't sweating. He wouldn't win, but that wasn't the point, he was fit, he looked handsome, ears cocked. Here was Robert in his own colours, in white and blue, in Mary's colours, goddamnit why couldn't Alice stop thinking of her husband in phrases she had picked up from her old lover. The stable boys turned the horses' heads in, here was Rainbow, she took off surcingle and blanket, Robert checked the girths. Among jockeys he was always the tallest; but that meant that he had to be the thinnest of the thin, she saw every cold muscle stir. The next thing she knew she was giving him a leg up, he grinned, he never said much.

Members' enclosure. Voices. Wind. Snow that wouldn't fall. How could she tell Kit she couldn't bear him being here, she had tried and tried but she wasn't strong enough, all she knew was that if he went away and never came back her throat would not always be dry and her eyes would not always be dry and aching, then wet and shameful, then dry and aching once more. She didn't want to tell him. She did want to tell him. Well, not now. Soon though. When she had a chance. The race, the race was the thing. Not that she could do anything about that either now. Anyway, after dinner Kit was driving down to town. But she must say something. Only cowards wrote letters. Couldn't just let him go, ignorant like that.

I'm gonna wash that man right outa my hair. Dear God why have I loved him so much? After loving him so much, how can I forget him for eternity, yes, for eternity, and have no other choice, no further chance, have mercy, no, don't, have strength.

When Rainbow was way back, coming past the stand, Alice felt Kit look at her worriedly. She didn't meet his eyes. She knew Robert was going to take it steady first time around. When the early leaders dropped back, when Rainbow started moving up through the field, she prayed the horse wasn't tired already, prayed the plan might work, they might get a place. When Rainbow fell she stood very still.

Alice felt Benedict give her his field-glasses. Out of focus. She twiddled the knob. Greys, greens, dizziness in double circles trying to get into one circle.

"Is Robert all right?"

That was Kit. What a fool question.

"Of course he's all right," she said drily.

Grass. Sky. Tops of cars. Fence. A loose horse, Rainbow.
St John's Ambulance uniforms. Robert getting to his feet.

"He's up," Alice said.

———◆———

After feeling Rainbow hit the birch fence. After going
down still holding the reins, after falling fast and hard and
Rainbow coming down and they skidded yards on the damp
grass and he lost the reins. After realising the horse hadn't
rolled on him, hadn't kicked him, the horses coming behind
had landed and galloped on and Rainbow had lain for a moment and then got up. After quiet coming back, and feeling
winded, sick, the St John's Ambulance men stationed by the
fence with their stretcher came over and asked Are you all
right? And he said Yes, hang on a minute, let me breathe, no
I can walk thanks, can you see my stick anywhere?

One found his stick, the other helped him up. One called
him sir, the other called him lad. They were both very
friendly.

Then the loose horse to catch, and trust his luck to fall
four fences out on the far side of the course with miles to
walk feeling groggy, no, somebody would give him a lift, a
good thing too, he was wearing the glorious new racing
boots Alice had bought him in Newmarket, the soles were
as thin as the cheque she had written, they'd be ruined if
he walked far. But first Rainbow. It would take the boy a
while to come from the loose-boxes to help.

The first wisdom from the ambulance men and the old
fellow who repaired the fences as to why the horse fell. Yes,
putting on the pressure – got to be among the leaders soon,
if you reckon to be in the race at all. No, not crowded, horse
saw the fence clear, just tired and ridden hard into it, too

hard, and we timed it wrong. And oh hell I was enjoying that, Alice will be disappointed, I had hoped for third place, when we came down third was possible, she worked for weeks getting the horse fit for this race.

Then Robert was sitting on a straw bale near the horse-box. He had put on a coat, but he still felt cold, the wet grass where he fell had soaked and stained his breeches, cold made him feel tired, suddenly dead tired. Whisky. A hot bath. Dinner. Not too much talk. Bed.

Dusk came. It might freeze tonight. Wind whined in bare thorns and oaks. Rainbow was groomed, he was rugged up, he looked none the worse for his fall. Alice led him up the ramp, Kit helped, he carried things, it was good to have Kit. Kit whose steadfast loyalty banished all superficial ills. Kit whose love for Alice wasn't bad, it uncovered evils maybe, but it was innocent. Alice whose love for Kit was . . . Yes, it was, wasn't it?

"You look white," Alice said on the tail-board. "Sit in the cab. I've nearly finished."

"Bit shaky still. I'm all right."

"Don't get cold."

Then they were up in the horse-box, he heard Rainbow's hooves on the boards, Alice's voice, Kit's voice, they didn't need his help, he felt too weary to move, went on sitting on the bale. When he was in a good humour, he knew their love was ornate and self-indulgent, it would quickly pass like all showy things. When he felt depressed, like now, he knew his love for Alice and hers for him wasn't admirably gentle, it was just weak – and shown up vilely by the other, grand thing.

"That bolt goes in here."

Alice was explaining how the horse-box partitions worked.

"Shall I get him a hay-net?"

"Yes, please. There's one there."

"Poor old Rainbow."

"*Come* on." That was Alice, softly. "*Come* on." Rainbow's tired hooves. "*Move* over, old boy. All right, Kit, bolt it please."

Their voices sounded muffled through wood. Muffled, but familiar, comfortable. He ought to stand up, try to get warm. In a moment he would. High in the slaty sky, rooks headed for a rookery.

"Have I tethered him too tight?"

"Er . . . Yes, I think you have. Hold on."

"Another time, I want to see Rainbow win."

And then the voices stopped. At first, Robert didn't realise. He thought how even if he had fallen in the Prince of Wales' Cup, he had won the Queen's Cup, and his father would have been pleased. But no sound came from the horse-box.

Robert stood up. Yes, it was true. No sound. Just Rainbow munching hay. So . . . Alice had shaken her head. There could be no doubt, Robert saw it plain. He had not been expecting this. Nor had Kit, no doubt, poor fellow. But – she had turned from the halter she was retying. She had met Kit's gaze in the wooden strawy gloom. She had shaken her head, faintly. And Kit had understood.

Robert felt shy, he moved away. He was stiff from bruises and from cold. He slapped his numb hands round his sides, stamped his frammed feet till they hurt, felt sluggish blood start to pump. Perhaps he had imagined wrong, perhaps . . . Can you never be contented if you know you are fallible? He saw the dark bulk of the feeding horse, night falling outside the oblong back of the horse-box; heard Kit say, Another time, I want to see Rainbow win; saw Alice smile, duck past Rainbow's head, saw Kit take her in his arms, watched her face come up to his. No, that scene was a travesty, his imagination laughed it off stage. But shameful performances were often hits . . . Yes – but not with these actors. Oh, actors will do anything. Those two are actors, you're not; they are moved by forces that don't move you. They're not meretricious. Perhaps they are meretricious. Are you sure you'd recognise the meretricious right before your face – what mastery of these distinctions do you command, a man shivering and shaking like you can't think.

The last cars and horse-boxes were jolting away down the track. Their side-lights were lit. Get a grip on yourself,

Robert cursed, to malign Kit is pretty shabby. And far more unjust – wretchedly ungenerous – was to send him away; for Alice had shaken her head, not kissed him, of that Robert now had no doubt. Almost he hurried back to the horse-box, almost he ran up the ramp into the murk where Rainbow tugged at his hay-net, almost he cried No, let's have Kit with us, damnit I don't want to lose him, and he doesn't deserve this.

He had to go back to the horse-box whatever he said. They'd think he was mad, wandering off. Alice didn't deserve this either – why did she have to punish herself so conventionally? Kit wasn't the snag; his banishment would serve no good end, was mean-hearted, should not be allowed. Abusing eloquent love doesn't do quiet love any good. Abusing wild love doesn't do tame . . . Oh for Christ's goddamned sake. It wasn't his marriage that Robert objected to, what do you expect of institutions, anyhow they can be altered; it was himself. Why couldn't the sky even snow for him when he felt like snow and the sky clearly felt like snow too? Come on, a blizzard, do something . . .

Back at the horse-box, Robert Clabburn climbed achingly into the cab. That had been a hard fall, why did he still feel so knocked about, he must be getting old, over thirty your steeplechasing days began to be numbered. Hell – whisky and a hot bath. Pity this machine had no heater. Alice climbed in beside him, switched on the engine, the lights. Kit walked round in front through the close-up glare of the headlights; his face looked hideously blanched, his eyes black holes; he swung up into the cab too. Robert said nothing, Alice let in the clutch.

At dinner, old Mrs Clabburn was coldly courteous to the man she had no doubt was her daughter-in-law's lover or wanted to be, who repaid years of hospitality with deceit. Robert Clabburn noticed and felt guilty.

Benedict Dobell didn't know what had occurred, but he sensed something had. Their three white faces gave them away, etiolated cheeks to which the logs blazing in the dining-room fireplace gave no colour, roast lamb and Burgundy and trivial talk gave no vivacity. Wearily he hoped that their loves might be moderate and their lives peaceful, it needed so little compromise, they didn't realise how lucky they were. That his daughter loved two men seemed to him completely unimportant. She was fortunate to love two such good ones, was his only reflection, and to be loved by them. Thérèse worried him more. Not that he saw her from year's end to year's end. But she wrote letters witty enough for her stepfather to be anxious that independence and dalliance might be getting too sophisticated for a naïve emotion like love ever to have its way, her melancholy too sharp, her scepticism too profound.

Beneath the table, Zampa stretched and sighed; her master felt her chin settle on his foot. At Durstead Hall, as at Fen House, the deer-hound was never dismissed to kennels, kitchens, cars. Dining-room and drawing-room were open to her, she stalked where she pleased, lay on the best Afghan rugs.

Above the table, Dobell took the decanter from his godson, went on talking about the Queen's Cup. But his mind skittered, he heard wind rattle shutters as it boomed along the lawn. Logs shifted, puffing up sparks; a gust made the chimney sough, a wisp of smoke wreathed into the room. An eighteenth-century marriage, that was what Alice and Robert needed – or was what they were getting whether they liked it or not . . . something profane and decorous. Was it after the Regency, did English marriage lose caste about the same time as English architecture? I am old and I have had heart attacks, he told himself, that may be why I find concentration hard. People took themselves so seriously when they fell in love – they were so personal.

Where was that detached woman he loved so much, that saviour of children's eyes? Walking about in Bangladesh. What time of day was it there? Standing in the wind on Fakenham Heath, that was what had made him so tired. And failing of his own hope for a romantic love until death in the Victorian or twentieth-century style had made him cynical.

Alice felt her face growing ugly as she had felt it in Milan. Thank God she didn't have to wheedle and flirt to get the damned thing's photograph on the covers of inane magazines these days. Robert looked ill. That was his fall, he had come down hard. Was it his fall? How could it be, he'd had nastier falls than that and gone dancing till dawn.

She hardly dared look at Kit, his eyes shone so bright, those eyes he said were the colour of dirty water, those eyes she had always delighted to watch change colour depending on the light and what shirt he wore.

Why did Robert talk resolutely with his mother and his father-in-law if he hadn't sensed that scene in the horse-box, if he didn't want to leave Kit to her? Or was it the civilised behaviour of the man who knows his wife's passion for his friend can come to no triumph and is trying to prevent it coming to a shameful defeat? Oh too late . . .

Why did mild love drive out intense, was it the same as bad money driving out good? Alice waited till Kit was looking away, turned to him, said silently and very calmly, said for the unrecorded record: I love you more than I can ever love anyone else, I will love you till I die. Forgive me if I do not look at you, if I met your eyes I should cry, so I shall look at that painting over there, beyond your shoulder. You see, Kit, the mediocre will always drive out the fine, the second-rate is victorious in me now. You can't complain, sweetheart, you helped weaken the first-rate, or did you preserve it? Yes, look at it like that, dear heart – if you had asked me to marry you, if you had merely let me love you, we would have degenerated. You didn't want that, so you cast me off and you were right. What was it Lampedusa wrote of love? Damned fine. You used to quote it to me, in

166

your tactful way. *Flame for a year, ashes for thirty.* Flame for a year if you're lucky I should say.

So I shall love my husband and our child. We may have more children. Kit, you make a mockery of other loves, I am a mockery of loves, forgive me, think of me kindly. The stupid thing is, it's probably too late for Robert and me, this marriage has learned too much from your love. But I'm tired. You must go please darling and never never come back. We'll always have Italy. Always, diminishing. Sound like Humphrey Bogart, don't I? You'll have to forgive me my cowardice – when you said you wanted to see the horse win another time, I saw my chance and grabbed it, that was the most trite action of my life. You knew Robert was outside, you couldn't say a word, you gazed at me, you turned away.

Kit Marsh thought, If that frumpish harridan allows discourteous inflexions to be audible in her voice once more, I'll get up and leave the room. Why doesn't Robert keep the old hag in a shed, I know he's trying to muffle her but even so, this isn't a dinner party it's a parish council meeting. I've been chewing the same mouthful for a good hour and a half, I think I may die an old man with this slice of lamb in my mouth, some evenings I can handle six righteous old women but tonight not one.

Still at the dining table, his last hour with Alice ticking away, Kit was already in his car driving down to London on icy roads. He'd let himself into his flat in the dead hours, try to sleep briefly, that was likely to be a success wasn't it, he'd go to work . . .

Then he was in Italy, Alice and he had been up at Spoleto a few days of tawny autumn trees and pale skies illuminated with golds, reds, blues, greens, like books of hours. They had gone for long walks in the valleys and over the scarps, had come back tired at evening to eat truffles and wild boar and drink a light white wine from those hills. Then on Lago Trasimeno the islands had loomed mysteriously in the mist that seeped on the water, gun-metal water that shimmered and slapped; the cedars round the noble houses had held out their ragged boughs dripping dew and mist. Egret rose from wading and flew away over the rowing boat trailing their white plumes, skinny white bodies and gangling white wings ghostly in the glistening air.

The hitch was, old mother Clabburn would feel confirmed in all her unimaginative bullshit if he lit a cigarette in the middle of dinner – before the cheese, for instance, there was a moment ideally suited to the smoking of a cigarette. Particularly when you would never see Alice again. Or Robert. And couldn't look at her now for fear of . . . For fear. Fear of. What? For fear of love. It sounded too grand. But he couldn't think of another word for it.

The other hitch was that the nearest decanter was empty. Most of it he had drunk himself. But that didn't stop him wanting more. Oh why had Alice given up? He had been so stupidly confident, but she had despaired. And how could he face life without Alice and Robert, there wasn't anybody else he loved, the years to come looked very drear. Fool that he had been, he had even dreamed they might ask him to be some kind of atheistic godfather to Rose, the dream had made him happier than he could recall without blushing, Christ what a pantomime. He heard Robert say, Here, Kit, take the other decanter, give Alice and yourself some more wine. Had Robert guessed? Why should he have guessed? Alice would tell him tonight in the drawing-room or in bed.

Robert had not put on his watch again after riding, he had no idea of the time. But it must be getting late, they were drinking coffee, he felt exhausted, soon Benedict would say he must drive home. Then poor Kit would feel he couldn't stay much longer. Probably he'd want to go. Be alone.

"Kit, shall we drink a glass of brandy?"

"Oh . . ."

Poor old lad, his eyes look desperate, Robert thought, he can't even decide if he wants a drink.

"Yes, let's have brandy." That was Alice. "Benedict, Kit, don't go yet."

"Everyone happy to drink it here?" Robert asked, standing at the sideboard hunting for suitable glasses. "No one want to go into the drawing-room? Fire's lit there too."

"We're all happy here," Alice said.

It was wet and dark in his head, Robert could feel despair growing like mould. He didn't want Kit and Alice sacrificed to him, they were fools if they thought he'd accept that. Since his marriage, which once he had dreamed was essential, had turned out to be a contingency, it held no value for him at all. Wrong. It held value as a way of stopping some judge awarding custody of Rose to her mother. Well, perhaps he could show them he knew how to out-sacrifice the sacrificers yet.

Robert walked round the table with glasses. Benedict had given Kit one of his cheroots. Just like the old days. Zampa's tail thumped sleepily.

He sat down with his own glass. One hip and knee were bruised from his fall, he shifted in his chair. Alice stood up, put a log on the fire. Sitting down again, she smiled at him nervously.

III

"When is Alice coming back?"

"Tomorrow evening." Robert glanced at the carriage clock which, after the obsequies for chaise and barouche, had a second life in a second century on the Durstead drawing-room mantelpiece. "No. Already it's this evening."

"And you want me to . . ."

"I want you to be here when she arrives." Trying hard not to sound weary, he explained again, "That's what I invited you for."

"Dear G-G-God, Robert, b-b-but have you the faintest idea . . ."

"Of course I have."

This time his irritation was audible, he saw Kit Marsh flinch. But why did he have to make such a fuss? Having with deliberation decided what he would do, having felt such happiness when everything was resolved, he found Kit's vacillation intolerable. Worse, he found it vulgar. And he was fastidious enough not to want to spend their last evening feeling his old friend was vulgar. Oh for God's sake, didn't friendship count for anything? He had imagined Kit would understand at once, would say Yes, certainly, I'll do it for you. He had imagined no more need be said. Perhaps he wasn't very imaginative. But nothing that had been said the last hour had needed saying. Why wouldn't Kit go to bed and leave him alone to muse?

"Have you written her a letter?"

"Yes." Did Kit seriously imagine he hadn't? "It's on her desk. But she'll need somebody. You're the person she'll need above all. She's wept on your shoulder before, hasn't she?" he asked, laconic in order not to sound harsh. "Perhaps you'd be kind enough to let her weep on it again."

"I'm not sure I . . ." Kit was fretting about the room. "Of course I *can*, but . . . Robert, I don't *want* to face her. I'm sure you think I'm a coward, but . . ." He said it as calmly as he could, but his voice had ugly quaverings in it that night. "I would very much rather not."

"But you understand that you have to. Do we need to discuss it any more?"

Kit flinched again. He knew Robert would rather he sat down. But he didn't feel like pretending he felt calm.

"Alice will never recover!" he nearly shouted. "Have you stopped caring for her? What you're doing is cowardly. Oh God, I'm sorry, I don't mean that."

"Think what you like," Robert said stiffly. "You may be right."

A green marble lamp, an ivory cigarette box empty because the Clabburns didn't smoke, a bottle . . . "May I?" Kit asked, taking out the cork, pouring his third glass of Armagnac.

Robert, who had drunk one glass after dinner, laughed his quiet laugh. "If you need it – by all means."

Alice had destroyed Kit last spring. For six months he had not left London, had worked every day and most nights – and had known how destroyed he was. Now it was autumn and Robert had telephoned and said, Alice is away for a few days, why don't you come up to Durstead and keep me company, I never said goodbye, anyhow I want to see you. So Kit had come. And now he was to be destroyed again, but by Robert this time. And he couldn't complain, because it was Robert that Robert was destroying, Kit would only be finished incidentally like any lesser thing involved in a greater ruin, Robert's destruction would dispel what wisps

171

of Kit's spirit Alice had spared that had prolonged a spectral life since spring. Couldn't protest, either. Though he had protested of course like a fool. For Robert Clabburn had gone about his farm these last months on foot, on horseback, in the Land Rover – and there on the fields where decisions are silent and solitary he had found himself detached from mother, wife, child . . .

"Of course I'll do what you want. But I shall never come back to Durstead. You understand that, don't you?"

"Don't make declarations like that," Robert murmured. Where had he got this wryness from? Kit wondered, hating it. Yes, he had changed. Here came the laconic voice again. "You can't know what things will look like next year – in five years' time . . . I hope you will often come back."

"For pity's sake, Robert!" There went his damned voice quavering again. "Without you I can never meet Alice again."

"You will tonight."

Do anything but this, Kit Marsh had cried, do any ludicrous thing: this, this alone, is intolerable. We'll put Rose in her cot in the back of the car, I'll drive you to Heathrow, you can leave on the next flight to Brazil, change every lousy thing, but live. Go to Recife. Go deep-sea fishing, play polo, backgammon can be fun, there's always the opera. I would leave Rose with Alice, Robert had said, for whom gestures had come to be more important than people, who therefore would act generously. Why Recife? I don't know why Recife, Kit had said, a man in a bar once told me it was paradise, probably it's hell. All right damn you, if you won't go to Recife, divorce Alice, I'll marry her, it'll be a farce of a marriage but that is insignificant, I swear blind you'll have Rose all you want. That's not it at all, Robert had said, it's not other people.

"What are you going to do?" Kit asked.

Both their minds went to the gun-room. Their ghost selves stood there side by side as their substantial selves had stood innumerable times. The walls were hung with riding whips, with sporting trophies, with coats. There were framed photographs of members of the family at race-meetings, at duck-decoys, at their weddings, in uniform. There were coloured engravings from the days when galloping horses were invariably portrayed with all four legs stretched out, a posture no horse ever took. Robert and Kit had stood there oiling dismantled shot-guns amicably. They both liked the smells of gun-oil and of the leather box where the cleaning gear was kept, they liked the gleam of guns standing in their glass-fronted case, the shapes of barrels and stocks and fore-ends laid on the oil-stained table. They both liked the fishing rods in corners, old coaching whips and powder flasks on shelves. They liked the cupboards crammed with skates, balaclavas, boxes of flintlock pistols, hunting knives, leather boots, swords and daggers from various countries and various wars, creels and gaffs, accumulations of years.

"I'm going to have a sailing accident. There's a tide in the morning."

"A *sailing accident?*" Kit Marsh laughed for the first time that night. "No one will believe in it."

"No one has to believe in it." Robert Clabburn crossed the drawing-room, drew a curtain, opened a window. He stared out across the lawn at the wind in the black wood. "Force three. Perhaps four."

"You can't have a sailing accident in a force three or force four. I could. But you can't."

"Maybe it'll pick up."

They both laughed. This was better, Robert thought, Kit had stopped whining.

"Robert . . ."

"Yes?" He finished closing the window, he turned. "I'm glad you've cheered up."

"When you d-d-die . . . The way you sail, they'll make you skipper of the *Flying Dutchman*."

"Oh . . ." He sounded surprised. Then the crow's-feet wrinkled round his eyes. "Oh . . . Thank you, Kit."

Toward daybreak, Kit threw his last cigarette into the fireplace, went to the kitchen, brewed a pot of coffee. The vigil was nearly past. Robert had been upstairs a long time, sitting by his daughter's cot. Then his footfalls came down the stair.

The kitchen was cold. One of the lurchers whimpered in its sleep, chasing insubstantial hares. The fridge neighed softly. They drank coffee, watched the watery greys and pinks begin over the russet trees, over the roofs of the farm.

"Kit . . . If you like . . . I can write a note for the girl to look after Rose for a few hours. The tide is high about eight o'clock. Do you want to come?"

<hr />

Stubbles had been ploughed, the wind whirled yellow leaves, hedgerow verdure had been beaten by rain. Kit Marsh tried not to think of his meeting with Alice that evening. And how would he face Mrs Clabburn when she discovered her son had talked to him through the night and then . . . That didn't matter – whether he could face people didn't matter at all. No, but it would be extremely unpleasant. And how would he face Rose, that unknowing bundle still asleep upstairs at Durstead Hall, how would he ever face Rose?

He watched Robert Clabburn drive, at each bend of the lane he was losing him, Robert was losing himself. No man can be required to live, that is tyranny. The Romans used to help each other do this. My help has been more sinister. I wonder if I mean that?

"I wish you wouldn't look at me like that," Robert said.

Benedict Dobell had sold Morston Manor when Emma died. The church stood as defiant and graceless as ever on its mound. The walled orchard whose trees Benedict had tended, where Kit and Alice had lain, looked uninviting in cold morning light as they drove by. Kit caught a glimpse of her attic window, then it was gone, he didn't say anything. He didn't believe Robert was filled with longing and regret as he himself would have been if he had had the forcefulness to bring his life to such a pitch of clarity. But what was consuming him then? Kit didn't understand. He'd have years to think about it. Yes – but already it was too late to know. He felt so stupid it made him want to cry. Here they were, they had arrived, he had done no good at all, his love was worthless. Robert didn't want to talk, why had he brought him? For silent companionship? An idiot scared dumb and jittery by someone else's death, a death this calm? Just to drive the car back? That was more likely, on that level Kit might serve.

Where the sail-shed had fallen down, and then for many years there had been nothing at all, a watch-house had been built, Kit couldn't think why, it seemed a shame. Fresh paint, balconies, notice-boards. Robert said at summer weekends now the whole place became a car park, there were charabancs, ice-cream vans. A public lavatory stood in some scrub.

Rigging *Whirlwind* down by the creek, they watched grey tide flooding in, chuckling round the anchored boats.

"Don't reckon I need the spinnaker," Robert said. "Nor these." He grinned, pulled out two life-jackets, chucked them aside with the boat-cover.

Not a fisherman, no one, only gulls. Just as well, perhaps, Kit thought. In summer the coast might be strange, in autumn it was itself, would be for a few years yet. Sound of the wind rapping halyards against masts. Cold of the creek when they launched *Whirlwind* and he stood in it over his knees, held her bow while Robert hoisted his sails.

"I hope this doesn't get you into trouble," Robert said gruffly through the flapping.

"I don't mind about that . . . that sort of thing . . ."

Robert nodded, went on coiling halyards. He adjusted the outhaul, the kicking-strap. Went aft, shipped the rudder and tiller.

"Right. I think I'm ready to go."

"I . . . Robert, I'll . . . I'll come with you, if you want."

Robert's blue eyes looked up steadily. The despised force three or four fluttered his roan hair. A puff of laughter blew away.

"And sail the boat back?"

"No. Not sail the boat back."

"No." Robert shook his head. "Thank you – but – no."

Then he snorted, grinned. "Good God no, certainly not. Look after Alice this evening. Like I told you to."

Kit expected the cannonade of his heart to die down then. But it didn't, it roared and exploded till there was no room in his chest for breath. Tide flowed round his legs. His hand on *Whirlwind*'s forestay cramped cold. A herring-gull screeched and dived. What was Robert saying?

"Push off."

Kit pushed. "Goodbye," he said voicelessly.

Robert was hauling in his sheets, lowering the centre-board. He glanced over his shoulder and smiled.

"Poor old Kit. Goodbye."

———◆———

At last he was away. Robert Clabburn felt his heart lift as *Whirlwind* cleared the first bend in the creek.

Kit had been difficult for a few hours, but then he had pulled himself together, he was all right, there was a lot of good in Kit. He had even offered to come too and . . . Well, it was a decent offer. Or maybe only moderately good. He must have known it would be turned down.

Benedict had sold *Trio* years ago, but she still lay in Morston creek, though on a different mooring. She no longer had a bowsprit. *Whirlwind* came seething by with a beam wind – it was a westerly – Robert sitting on the gunwhale. He had cleated his jib sheet, though at every bend of the creek he had to free it and cleat it again. He played the main with one hand, the tiller-extension with the other. He had to spill a lot of wind because he was too light a crew, a Fourteen is tricky on your own. Alone! He had never been sufficiently alone. There had always been his family and the farm. To be amiably married, to be amiably divorced . . . What a deadly choice, he didn't want either.

A run down the next leg, but no gybe. A lot of the boats of his boyhood had vanished over the years, sunk or broken up. Where was *Sea Pink*? Where were *Bittern* and *Snark*? *Vanity* was still in her accustomed place; her varnish glistened in the morning sun, went matt when a cloud came. Where the Clabburn and Dobell moorings had been, no boat now belonged to any of them.

Tacking down the harbour, after long oppressed months he felt free. What was there to be afraid of? Nothing. Nothingness. Nothing at all. Astern, Cley windmill held out white bony arms. Was he afraid? he wondered. No – just nervous, the same nervousness he had before a race.

Spray on his mouth was good. One of the fishing-smacks had men on board. But that didn't matter, he would sail far out. Wind in his hair and eyes was good, quietness was best of all, quietness and solitude, horizon widening as he headed out to sea. Quiet . . . he'd never speak again. Here was a remedy for self-disgust. Good, oh wonderfully good. Which way should he sail? East, church tower by graveyard by tower – Cley, then Salthouse, then Weybourne mill, Beeston church, Cromer church, on? West beyond Wells to Holkham where on the sandy shore sometimes he had exercised horses? Once he had been bucked off into the shallows, he laughed remembering, laughed again to think he wouldn't laugh again.

Robert sailed out beyond the marshes where Kit and Alice had walked as lovers summer after summer. Where he had come himself with Cambridge lovers – he could hardly bring to mind their faces and names. They had meant little enough, girls who looked pretty in the car driving to Norfolk on May evenings, girls to ride with, dance with, make love with. High spirits and free time were all they had meant, what vanity, he should be ashamed. No, he should be grateful, the vanity was all that convinced you you were alive. Marshes where later he had walked with Alice and had asked her to marry him. She had shivered and gazed around nervously, he had not understood, there wasn't a soul for miles, there never was, just a baitdigger trudging far off, and then she had said Yes and smiled. Where now he came to free himself from that – and free her – she'd have to learn to like being free – and to make amends.

Not to have loved enough . . . That was unforgivable. Was it? It was if you allowed yourself to talk of love, or to marry. Not enough? Everyone was guilty then. But he was more guilty than most. Desperate enough to bolt from the ennui of fraudulent years, affection miscalled love, habit lulling to brutish contentment, all the lies . . .

Rose would never remember him. While she was a babe in arms, he could still go free. She would never grieve except abstractly, he was quits, he would be quits in an hour. Alice would have enough money. Thank heaven for a few hundred acres. She and Kit would compromise or they would not, it made no odds either way. The slapping of waves against the hull was finer than anything a priest or a notary could fix you up with. High mackerel cloud crossed the sun, veils of brown and grey and green light hung from the sky. Then it blew clear, the humped dunes *Whirlwind* passed gleamed goldenly with dark green marram crests; the sun splashed gold and silver paint on the sea and mixed them up; the sky was the palest blue wash Robert had ever seen. Don't blame the officials, it's not your wife you can't stand living with, it's your heart. Look at the tide rumpling in over the sandbanks, cormorant flying black and ragged and low, is that a redshank, yes I think so.

Here were the seals, Alice's seals, swimming in the blustery harbour mouth. Happy the seals. Happy the man who did not clutch at life, abjectly hoping that with time and obtuseness his unhappiness might fade. Happy the man who does not repeat himself, who plays his music once and if it was not brilliant that is of no consequence, it is dishonourable to come back on stage. Happy the man who takes no steps that he should be happy. What the hell do you mean by that, you're making yourself happy now in your somewhat perverse fashion, your heart is beating excitedly, yourself happy and others wretched, let's get this quite straight. Happy the man who has better things to serve than his own well-being, better things to save than himself. I think that's enough rhetoric, why don't you enjoy your sail. You're serving nothing and saving nothing. You just like the quiet sounds of wind on sails and hull on sea, this soughing, this lilting, this peace.

Fighter aircraft swept low overhead, their black shadows racing over the waves, their maddening howl coming after them. Suddenly Robert Clabburn felt depressed, he didn't understand why. Then he remembered, once he had even thought it might be good for Alice to marry him. Alone at sea in cold wind he blushed, sweat slid on his face. No, he didn't want to live with that.

Whirlwind reached through the chop outside Blakeney Point. Her sails were the only sails. Offshore, a coaster steamed. Over the foreshore, over the sea, oystercatcher and tern fished. The aeroplanes had disappeared, their screaming died in his head, his sweat dried.

East? West? Robert didn't want to go anywhere, he kept sailing north straight out to sea. The green cone of Wreck buoy dropped astern. The grey sea had greenish and bluish lights, a few white horses broke. It was good stuff, the North Sea, he had always liked it. He studied its lumpish surfaces, its heaving and chucking, the spray his boat made. Yes, it would do the trick, it would do fine.

After half an hour, the land was dim, it lay along the south horizon like an arm laid on a sill. It was a pity his depression and shame had come back like that, he was afraid now. Couldn't help it. Natural. Not that it would make any difference. Perhaps if he sailed on, his heart would lift again.

Sailing had never failed him yet. There was no hurry. He was free. Might as well go a good long way.

FIVE

I

"There's Benedict." Alice Clabburn stopped her car on the Fen House drive. "There's your grandfather. Can you see him?"

Rose pushed herself up from the car seat, craned her neck, gazed at the wood, the yard. "Where? Where?" she cried.

Alice leaned and pointed.

"Benedict!" Rose shouted when her eyes found him, though he was too far off to hear.

Her mother opened the car door, Rose jumped out and ran over the rough grass into the orchard trees. "Benedict!" she shrilled again. A tussock brought her down sprawling – but luckily not on a thistle. She picked herself up, toiled on with her wobbling childish run.

Benedict Dobell was scything among his fruit trees, mulberry and medlar and quince. He had scythed all his life; he did it with an accurate swing few younger men were trained in, a swing he used to keep up all afternoon and could still manage for a quarter of an hour. Then he would rest, leaning on his scythe.

Putting her car in gear again, Alice saw her father prop his scythe against a plum tree, take up his blackthorn walking-stick, make a few steps toward his rushing stumbling granddaughter. A tawny patch in the grass stirred; with slowness like her master's, a very nearly dead deer-hound heaved onto her feet, feebly wagged her tail. Alice watched the child come face to chest with the dog, face to thigh with the man. She hesitated till she saw that neither Benedict, nor Rose, nor Zampa – all equally unsteady on their feet – had during their embraces fallen on the scythe. Then she drove on to the yard through the neglected garden.

Benedict might scythe a path here or there, but the demesne was no longer under man's dominion – not that he resented this in the slightest, his daughter knew. There was no gardener any more, which meant that roses were rarely pruned (and then only those an aged man could reach) and that lawns were never mown. Now in June, what in Emma's time had been sward was hay field. Dappled feathery heads waved in the westering sun, pollen flecked the light. Flower beds had become thickets. The posts and rails of deserted paddocks had rotted, some had fallen. Outhouse roofs needed repairing; the gutters had blocked with dead fledgelings, grass, leaves; damp had wormed into the brickwork. A flycatcher had made her nest in an old wrought-iron lantern. Wrens had nested in a crack in the masonry.

The house itself was in reasonable condition – Dobell spent what he could afford on running repairs to the main building – but there too window-sills were decaying, would have to be replaced one day. A woman still came from the village once a week to sweep and dust. On occasion Alice would conspire with her by telephone from Durstead, and then a pie or a cake would be left on the kitchen table. Her car was packed with provisions now, she never arrived unladen, tonight they would all want dinner . . . But for the most part her father subsisted on game stew all winter, salad from a surviving patch of kitchen garden all summer, bread and Stilton all year round, bottles of Guinness and of Bordeaux – the cellar was still well stocked with wine.

The scything was not resumed. Benedict hobbled back to the yard leaning on his blackthorn, scythe over his shoulder. The child carried the whetstone, using both hands. The deer-hound ambled along.

"Can we go rowing?"

He had forgotten to scythe the path to the boathouse that year, the rushes must be head-high.

"We'll see if we can fight our way down there," he said to the blonde head stumping along at his side. "You'll need boots. And a stick to hack through the carr."

Also he had forgotten to launch the skiff. She was lying upside-down by the staithe. Certainly she would leak. The rushes would grow through her next year if she wasn't moved. The remaining sound planks would rot next year if she wasn't painted. He wondered if he was still capable of hauling the boat into the water. Probably not. They would need help. He would have the skiff put to rights, he mustn't forget, then Alice could teach the child to row.

"Can we feed the ducks?"

"That's a good idea. There's a mallard on the lily pond with ducklings. We'll take a scoop of corn. But come and have your tea first. Have you forgotten who's here today?"

"How many ducklings?" Rose wanted to know.

"Seven or eight, I believe."

That would be splendid, Rose knew where the tin scoop lived in the meal-bin in the stable, she would fetch it at once. No she wouldn't, she remembered she couldn't lift the meal-bin lid. Anyhow, they would set off from the terrace into the long grass that fluttered and sighed over her head, that was full of thistles and poppies, alive with things that churred and things that hummed, things that flitted and crawled. She would carry the tin scoop with corn for the ducklings.

They would go past the yew trees, they would make their usual jokes about not falling into the ha-ha. Perhaps she would jump into the ha-ha. Then there would be the silver birches, the lilies, dragonflies and ducklings, moorhens and daddy-long-legs. Perhaps she would see one of the bream turn over near the surface, or water-boatmen skittering about, or a water-rat. There would be a lot of frogs, the weed would stir in streamers and wreaths, the freshwater would smell of sun.

Rose Clabburn stood unnoticed in the door of the drawing-room. Who was the strange lady sitting on the ottoman listening to Mummy? Greeny gold sunlight cascaded through the windows. The faded yellow wallpaper stood golden in healthy patches, colourless in mangy patches. The dazzle was confused with the faint smells of tobacco and flowers. The yellows got confused with the miraculous red and green dress the strange lady wore.

The child blinked, otherwise she didn't move. Green leaves of the roses in vases on the mantelpiece, on the piano, on the marquetry table whose inlaid peacocks and doves she had been introduced to and that she liked. Red and white and yellow petals. Green leaf and shiny white flower of the magnolia in a cut-glass bowl on her dead grandmother's bureau. Sleepiness of the shimmer on a walnut tall-boy. Sleepiness of the tick of the dilapidated French clock that didn't tell the time. The odd way nothing looked like it looked like in the curving looking-glass . . .

Still, at least the sea-horse on the top looked like a sea-horse. Rose would know a sea-horse when she met one, in the sea or in a dream. The odd way some bits of paintings were so gloomy she could make nothing out, other bits were easy to understand. A rider's red leg on a grey horse. Then, across the room, an angel blowing a trumpet. By the far door, a cottage that looked enticing, a muddy path, some windy trees. The angel couldn't be Norfolk, but the muddy path might be. It was bewildering, because sometimes she was almost certain she had seen things in a picture that didn't seem to be there next time she came; but instead she would see things that must have been hiding in the gloomy bits last time, but now had come into the light.

Zampa's slow tread crossed the hall, she pushed gently past Rose, headed for the hearthrug. What were Mummy and the lady mardling about? she wondered without making the effort to listen to the words.

The red and green dress turned, there was a shadowy smile, the dress stood up. Rose approached, still blinking. The sun caught her on the side of her face. Its slope of light falling across the room had uncountable motes of dimness and brightness sliding down it. The slanting brilliance angled across the strange lady so she could not be seen.

"Darling, come and meet Thérèse."

Alice saw her sister's green eyes light up; saw her weary mouth lift; saw with what modesty she lightly took the child's shoulders in her battered hands, how faintly she kissed the top of her head.

When Benedict had taken Rose to attend to the ducklings, Alice finished what she had been saying.

"Yes," she muttered bitterly, "Robert left me a letter. But it didn't say a bloody thing. He was sorry. It was all his own responsibility. It wasn't that he didn't love Rose and me, but . . . Oh Christ, you can imagine, can't you? The conventional bullshit I had thought we were beyond."

"Yes . . ." Thérèse said as blankly as she could. Nothing would be gained now if her voice betrayed how dull she had found Robert Clabburn. But she heard that damned inherited drawl of hers, so she said it again, swiftly, lightly, superficially, "Yes."

"He hoped I might marry again. Hoped I would forgive him. Oh nothing that meant anything . . . I felt humiliated. I still do."

"He was, perhaps," remarked Thérèse, feeling more generous, "a very conventional man – who came to hate himself. And found, at the end, unusual honesty, unusual courage. Do you think even, at the end, an unusual pleasure?"

Alice was afraid she would ask her about that autumn night when she drove home to Durstead and found Kit but no Robert.

"And Kit – do you ever see him?"

"I . . ." Alice turned back her wrists, opened her palms in helplessness. "For two years he wouldn't come near me. Wouldn't talk on the telephone. Wouldn't answer letters. Then I persuaded him this was ridiculous. Made him confess Robert had hoped he would come here. So . . . We have tried seeing each other. We have tried leaving each other be. When he's present, he's absent."

"Oh . . ." Thérèse drawled, "he was always that."

Alice laughed too, gratefully. She sniffed, swallowed.

"Yes. And when he's away – I find him everywhere, he never leaves me. Poor Kit! It makes no difference what he does."

"Poor Alice," her sister said. And then, "I should like to see him."

Thérèse sauntered to the window. Wistaria had grown across the panes. Dandelions and groundsel had sprouted through terrace bricks; an urn had tipped over, spilled earth and some withered plant now overcome by weeds. Gnats jittered. Down by the lily pond, Benedict waded through long grass; his granddaughter and his hound could only be traced by the ruffling they made. Over the distant wood, a tatterdemalion heron flapped.

"It's good to be home." Thérèse laughed. "Do you know where this place reminds me of? Abbot's Hall."

———◆———

When her sister and her niece left after dinner, Thérèse strolled in the overgrown garden. Her dress swished pleasingly through dewy grass beneath the lime trees.

England in the nineteen eighties was hardly an attractive spectacle – why was she so contented to be back? Jingoism and avarice run riot, by God – and yet – and yet . . . The triumph of bourgeois Philistia – neither the humanitarian Thérèse de Nérac nor the Bohemian could feel at home. But still – on a summer night she didn't care, other states in which she had lived were more ignominious still.

Was it just that alone in a wilderness on a remote coast – back in your privilege again, eh? – materialism was impotent? The sky was clear. Moon and stars lit palely on the creamy flower of the old-man's-beard that had overwhelmed an apple tree years ago. Now it had pitched its canopy over the holly tree beside it too. Turning a thickety path, she met a garden Artemis, white stone gleaming against dark foliage. Artemis was patting her small stone dog. Thérèse patted the dog too. If private amusement keeps a few people sane amid the public shame, don't mock it too virtuously, it may give up and die.

She recollected a marquee. Not the one put up for that absurd wedding. A marquee of her childhood, supernaturally grand and white it had been. For what party had it been ordered? Or for a fête? Afterward, Alice and she had taken camp-beds and sleeping-bags into the silvery cathedral. They lay awake whispering in the darkness and the smell of trodden grass and the breeze in the guy-ropes and flaps. She woke early in the morning, swallows came swooping in, a thrush hopped about. And thirty years later she came by worrying about hospitals in a mess, schools and universities shot to hell. Oh what a lousy pity, what a decline.

Benedict Dobell was in the library, knickerbockers and shooting stockings stretched to the fire, cheroot in hand. She accepted the glass of port he offered her.

"Tell me, when you found your father . . ."

Thérèse looked around at the leather bindings, the tusks, the Chinese jar of potpourri. Among the pictures, Tiepolo's Death still held audience. The Manton flintlock over the fireplace had been joined by a pin-fire fowling-piece inherited from Sam Mack (after decades of watching it rust, Dobell could now oil it as much as he liked). Zampa dozed on a rug. Thérèse laughed aloud – Benedict was her father, didn't he realise? Still, though Gilles de Nérac could not be remembered or loved, he could be honoured; and she had gone to honour him.

"Yes, I found him. I had visa trouble getting into the country. But I managed in the end. You can imagine – an old French graveyard near Hanoi."

They were both thinking of Gilles' widow buried a generation afterward in Tunstead churchyard under a later name. Thérèse carried the decanter to her stepfather, filled his glass, stood still beside his chair. She laid her hand on his shoulder. Almost every evening for years he had sat alone in the library reading and musing; she was glad she had come back while he was still alive.

"You're getting very like Dr Mack," she said.

"Am I?" Dobell laughed. "I am luckier than he was, I have you."

"Perhaps I am like him too, coming back to doctor in Norfolk." She squeezed his shoulder, let it go. "You can be old Sam Mack now. I'll be him later."

"And until then . . . ?" Anything was better than contemplating how solitary she was – far more isolated far younger than he had been. How she was not in love with anyone; she was probably too old ever to have a child; her friends were scattered about the globe. "I don't need looking after, you know."

"Shall I live here? I'd like to. May I live here?"

"My dearest girl . . ." He felt his face flush with pleasure, felt tears in his eyes; he had thought he would never feel such things again. "Dull for you," his voice stumbled.

"It's a big house. I won't get in your way."

"I would be enormously happy. But what will you do? Apart from ministering to the local coughs and broken legs."

"I'll plant trees." Her voice danced. "In ten years, I'll read my way through this library. On winter afternoons I'll shoot pigeon and duck."

"Would you . . ." Benedict ransacked his mind, suddenly he saw the decayed paddock rails. "Would you like me to . . . It's your birthday next month, isn't it? Can I give you a horse?"

"Yes," Thérèse answered happily, "I would accept a horse."

At two o'clock in the morning, Thérèse entered her bedroom upstairs. She stood irresolute at a window, then dropped into a chair.

The being delighted to be home had gone. It would come again. But it had gone. And now . . . In her letters to Benedict she had told him of the countries she had worked in, other countries she had visited when she was free. In his letters to her he had written exactly the news she liked to read, telling of seasons and neighbours, a book or an engraving he had bought, the peacocks, the bats, the hares. They had kept their melancholy to themselves, though each could imagine the other's.

She had not told him how the useless bustle, the vulgar falsity of human life dejected her. Of the tedium of a profession, any profession, for a man or woman of imagination. She had not told him because she knew he had felt it and understood – and, like all of us, he had hoped his depressing experiences were somehow unique and that those he loved might never share them. Nor of the futility of trying to be cheerful telling yourself that what you do helps other people. Nor of the futility of that principled help itself. Nor of the self-hatred that grows with years of squandered energy, self-hatred foully intensified when you let yourself forget your energy is squandered and then you remember again. Nor of the endless treading water, the self-deception that is half unconscious and half deliberate – any lie to keep the child of conscience quiet and the adult of habit functioning. Nor of a few inspiring passions that were transient, but while they lasted made her honoured and delighted to be alive; some modest affections that lasted, but by lasting never let her forget how lacklustre she was.

Thérèse went down to the kitchen for brandy . . . brandy for lucidity and calm now, brandy for sleep later with any luck . . . She lit one of her Gitanes. The scrubbed beech table glimmered white as a holy-stoned deck.

Back upstairs through the quiet darkened house. The grandfather clock ticked, she trailed fragrances of her French scent, her French spirit, her French tobacco. Half French, half English, that had always made her laugh in an exasperated way, she was half this and half that, oh irrevocably half-and-half.

In her room again, she heard the music she wanted to play on her record-player. Singing wordlessly, almost soundlessly, she flicked through a row of records, it was by Satie, where the devil was it . . . no, it might wake Benedict.

Ancient cities she had described in letters, temples of many faiths and architectures she had described, tropical islands she had described, hospitals and lack of hospitals she had described. She had told Benedict she had found

191

Gilles' grave . . . She had not told him yet, but she would, how she had haunted graveyards on the Bay of Bengal, on the Andaman Sea, on the South China Sea.

How through years, without knowing why, she had half forgotten it was one particular European's grave in Asia she wanted to find — how other graves had possessed her. She had pushed through undergrowth in Burmese hill-station churchyards, reading innumerable names and dates, dreaming how Shan incantation and the jungle Nats charmed dead officers and their wives, dead privates, padres, amahs, boys and girls. Meandering in India from Kerala to Sikkim, she had fed upon snatches of stories on memorials in dilapidated churches. All the dripping luxuriant greenery where, struggling and giggling, she had tried to enlist one of the browsing Hindu sacred cows to eat her a passage to some entangled monument whose cracked inscription she wanted to read . . . Then she got sick of British tombs. She went through ridiculous trouble to locate those few French cemeteries that still existed. Then, even more difficult, often in fact impossible, she went after the phantasmal Portuguese and Danes . . . On then to Malaysia, to Indonesia . . .

Melaka had been a turning point. In the ruined church on the hill overlooking the muddy river, the schooners, the strait, she had read gravestones in Latin, in Portuguese, in Dutch, in English . . . there were even Armenians there. Then she had gone down into the town, climbed up the other hill, Bukit China, and tried unsuccessfully to read the Chinese tombs. After that, she sought out graves of all races and faiths, wherever she fetched up in East Asia. Going to Vietnam to look for her father didn't stop her. Several years later when she found herself in Shanghai, she was still a crow flapping around tombs, her head an encyclopaedia of strangers' deaths, stories she imagined. Only converts did not appeal to her. Indians or Chinese who became Christians — if their motives were venal she despised them, if their motives were doctrinal she despised them even more. So too Europeans who became Taoists or this or that — they were guilty of taking the soul seriously, she convicted them of bad taste.

192

That was all over now. Her Asian ghosts would have to stand back, just as her surviving patients would have to turn to other doctors. Even . . . there lay, under the frangipani trees in the old graveyard at Penang, a youngish woman – she haunted Thérèse more than Gilles did. An English name, but she had been born in France. She had quite a big crumbling monument from the last century. No mention of a husband, of children – there she lay . . .

Now Thérèse would content herself with the North Walsham dead. She would take up her practice there soon, where as a child she had gone with her mother every market day.

Emma had driven the five miles from Fen House to North Walsham the last time . . . Several neighbours later recalled having seen her walking by the church, in the square. She had said Good morning to them. She had bought nothing. And on the way back – she must have been going seventy miles an hour round the bends in Westwick wood, the police declared – her car had skidded into the trees.

Thérèse finished her brandy. She must try to sleep. Under her bed, Sam Mack's box of bones waited.

II

A couple of old tyres at the heart of the bonfire. Spars of sycamore – Thérèse had done some copsing – still too sappy to blaze up. A willow, demolished by a storm the winter before and therefore sere now, not that willow ever burns well. Branches from pruned fruit trees, lop and top. Brushwood, thorn from hedgerows, a broken hive.

Rose picked up sodden sticks from the tussocks beneath an oak tree, carried them to the pyre, flung them at its flanks. It was sad under the oak tree, Zampa's grave was there, the soil still bare. Light drizzled through the gnarled branches. Flaps of brown and white fungus grew on the bole. Still, at home at Durstead the lurcher bitch was going to have puppies, Alice had promised they would keep one.

A garden table – waterlogged, mossy, with splinted legs, the home of innumerable woodlice – had been set up near the bonfire. On it stood buckets of earthy sand. "Let me help!" cried Rose. "Let me! What's this?" Her mother was taking fireworks from a box, sticking them in the bucket. Magical, the names they bore – Roman Candles, Chinese what was it ... Rose rummaged in the box. "What's this?"

"It's a Catherine Wheel. It spins round and round."

"Where does it go?"

"Here," Kit Marsh said. "This post will do fine."

The death of Benedict Dobell had fallen before he could buy Thérèse a horse; no repairs to the paddock had been made; but some uprights still stood. Kit took the Catherine Wheel from the shy child. No, she wasn't shy. But he was practically a stranger, she was shy with him. He took a hammer, a six-inch nail. Bang, bang, bang, bang . . .

He started remembering Venice, Alice going to the opera at the Fenice wearing a blue silk dress he had loved, her Magdalen's fair head and blue eyes on the pillow at night, necklace and earrings not yet taken off. How through the open window they heard the sleepy slapping of the canal, lamplight stippled the water, the reflections of moored skiffs quivered upside-down. Then he remembered an article on Bellini he once wrote. Bang, bang, bang. Then that his museum was broke, sacking people, he was losing his job. Thud. That was his finger. Damn. He flicked the Catherine Wheel, it twirled freely. He jiggled the six-inch nail. Bang, bang.

"There you are," he said to the child watching him. "When we light the fuse, it will go whirling round. Now, come and help me set up the rockets. And you must decide which ones you want to launch first."

The child for whose father's death he felt himself responsible . . . Every time his thoughts steadied on one probable interpretation, they then began to destabilise it. London year after London year this went on; he supposed he just had that cast of mind; he couldn't think of one possibility without following it with a second, a third . . .

Kit had not waited for what was left of Robert Clabburn to come ashore a few days later and a few miles along the coast, had not waited for fragments of *Whirlwind*. He was ashamed of the concealed hysteria and the helplessness of his last night with Robert. He was more ashamed of the revealed hysterical passions of the following night. And ever since, he had lain awake at night in London, tumid grey waters sloshing in his skull, tricklings and drippings of the brain driving him mad . . . till often it seemed the very act of thinking dispelled conviction, to phrase a feeling was to make it ring false. And what was there to brood on? Liver and lights of an old passion. Giblets of desire. Chitterlings, scrag . . .

The emblem of his guilt was busily lifting waxen, brightly coloured rockets from their box, laying them on the soaked grass. He explained to her that was a bad idea, showed her how to fix the rockets in the lengths of iron piping he had beaten into the ground, that stood slightly slanting so the rockets would soar away from the garden, harmlessly drop their charred sticks and tatters in the fen.

Are you lucky or unlucky, Kit wondered of his helper, that you're not growing up in Recife? And did your father intend me to be your stepfather? Alice Clabburn had long ago convinced herself that was what her dead husband had wanted . . . And Kit Marsh, who had convinced himself of myriad incompatible truths, recalled Robert saying he hoped he would often be at Durstead. But he recalled too the unfamiliar irony he had heard in his friend's voice that night. It was difficult to believe Robert cared what happened to any of them. Not even you, Kit murmured to the red woollen hat on the strawy locks by his legs. No, not even you.

Down the water-meadow, in the fifth of November scudding wind, Thérèse de Nérac was clearing a ditch, dydling a ditch they call it in Norfolk. She had been heaving at the long heavy crome for an hour, dragging out mud and weed, trying to get the black slime to flow and drain the land. Where she had dydled, the ditch trickled blackly. Black ramparts of dead rush, dead reed, mud, sticks, lay along the bank. Her feet slithered, her shoulders ached. She swung the crome, its curved tines sank into sludge, she hauled.

Weary while you do these things, more weary when you rest. It doesn't stop you fretting, but you fret less effectively. Try to cure the sick on working days. Struggle with thicket and marsh, sheds and orchard and garden on holidays. Read at night.

All autumn she had sawn logs on the saw-bench outside the wood-shed, glancing at the water-butt overflowing after rain, at an injured pear tree that leaned on its crutch in the wet grass like Long John Silver without his parrot. Every autumn evening she had lit a fire in the library (the drawing-room she had deserted till mild weather returned in May) and thought of her sister at Durstead Hall who also cut wood by day and burned it by night.

The squalls of rain that whipped the library windows at Fen House, a door that slammed, loosened soot that pattered down the chimney, a tawny-owl's tuwhit tuwhoo – Thérèse liked the sounds of her solitude. The same squalls beat through the beeches and limes at Tunstead where in their beloved churchyard the two sceptics lay side by side. She would lie there too one day unless . . .

If she lived to be old, she might go off on her wanderings again, she could give her half share of Fen House to Rose, she could leave for Sulawesi once more . . . Well, that was a decision that could wait, she had twenty years as a country doctor to do first. She must renounce her solitude a little too. Not much, but a bit. The odd dinner party wouldn't hurt. Though she hadn't lived in Norfolk since she was a girl, people remembered her; invitations were things that could be accepted as well as refused. It was just that sometimes on stormy nights she descended the staircase as fragmented as Duchamp's nude, so merely conjecturally did she exist.

She must remember to choose a box of children's books to go to Durstead Hall. Rose liked being read to, she had decided she was Mowgli her mother said. The Fen House nursery bookcases had been filling up since the last century, Thérèse had loved the touch of Victorian covers, the smell of Victorian pages. The illustrations to E. Nesbit novels had been the casements through which she had vanished to a past from which she could comprehend how she derived. Her views on horses had been formed by *Black Beauty*, on dogs by *Jock of the Bushveld*, on the English Civil War by *Children of the New Forest*, on American education by *What Katie did at School*. Whether a child might enjoy any of these now she had no idea. She would go up to the abandoned nursery one evening, shiver in the cold, smell the damp, sit on the rocking-horse, read a few pages here and there.

Cock-cock-cock of a pheasant going up to roost in the

wood. Thérèse hauled on her crome, in the gloaming a plover flew by. A wrench, a stagger, she dumped dripping mire on the bank, swung her crome groping into the ditch again. In a minute she would go and help with the fireworks and the fire – if she was never to be a mother, she could at least provide amusement for her niece on Guy Fawkes' Night . . . and Kit Marsh, she suspected, felt less ill at ease when not left too long alone with Alice and Rose.

Poor devil, Thérèse reflected, what was Kit doing visiting Norfolk, he hadn't a clue. Alice coaxed on the telephone – he wanted to be loyal to Robert Clabburn's ghost, but what was loyalty? – he loved Alice with all his heart, or he had believed he had . . . So after twisting and turning for months, he'd come up to Durstead for two or three nights – to do what? to be who? To go down to London again hating himself worse each time?

Kit in Norfolk had always been as nervous as a horse on board ship. Since Robert's death he was as nervous as a horse on board ship in a gale. And how should he not be? Maybe that suicide was brave and generous. Thérèse de Nérac knew enough about despair to respect a man who judged himself harshly; knew enough about the damned pack of hyenas called human society to admire a man who declined to go on eating offal year by year. Maybe that suicide was cruel and selfish . . . When the fool found he couldn't live up to his ideal, he made sure he wasn't going to have to think about it, or try to do better. Whatever that suicide was it finished Kit.

You only had to look at his scrawny arms and legs, scrawny chest, hollow cheeks, hollow eyes, thin hair. Yes, Kit was going bald, she had teased him about that. Still, Alice would not mind that his forehead looked increasingly grand. Loyal little wretch, my sister, Thérèse thought gruffly.

Robert got clear away without knowing what it is to be unfit, let alone unhealthy: truly a straightforward man leading a straightforward death. Never knew what it is not to be able to think what you want to think, stop thinking maddening things. How do I know? Never knew what it is not to be able to want what you want, feel what you dream you feel, mean what you think. Kit Marsh, by the gaunt look of him, knew all too well. That's right, insult the dead, sympathise with the living who helped bring them to death.

The reek of marsh gas soaked her brain – *ignis fatuus* when it burns, a stench otherwise. Still, after choking on exhaust on the streets of Manila and Bangkok it smelled all right.

When the last of the marsh gas wisped out of her grey-matter, Thérèse found she was in tears. God Almighty, what was this? She swung her crome again, her hands on the brown shaft were deathly white with black mud splotches, the blowing light was grey.

"Thérèse!" That was Rose calling. "Thérèse! Fireworks!"

In her ancient green and brown clothes now filthy grey, with her face that was grey as usual and her hair starting to go grey, Thérèse shouldered her crome, tramped through the scrub. A robin perched on the brown tangle of an elder tump; that red breast was cheering. Gulls straggling inland high overhead were sad though. She remembered her ear-rings, they were her mother's emeralds, along with the robin they must be the only brilliant things in the twilight, she smiled recalling the harness chest.

Bad feeling, not to be able to help. And worse not to know what issue to hope for – to bring Kit and Alice together in your mind, separate them, bring them together, separate them once more . . . Worse still to conclude that no future could be happy, there were no good possibilities. That was the blasphemy some had courage for and some had not.

Anyhow the wind was drying her eyes. A cypress by the stream, a laurel in the edge of the covert, writhed in a gust. The bare deciduous trees only quivered, they were made of harder stuff.

Friends in America, Kit had said, not a bad gallery, they'd give me a job I think. New York? No . . . (laughing) he'd be buried in the Mid-West. Have you ever, she had asked as lightly as she could, ever thought of farming in Norfolk? Usual Kit blushings and stammerings. Oh Thérèse I'm too melancholy to be much of a husband, don't you think? Well, yes, I do, but . . .

Thérèse watched her sister kneel on drenched grass to

shove dry newspaper and kindling into apertures in the bonfire. Alice's career as a rich and beautiful young widow had no doubt had its comic moments – but she was least discontented wearing Benedict's ravelling shooting coat that was too big for her, lighting a handful of straw to start the fire.

Kit was showing Rose how to make a spill to light fireworks.

"Look, there's the moon coming up. I'll light the spill. Hold it steady. Then see if you can shoot the moon."

Dear God, Alice thought, now Rose will fall in love with him. She saw her enchanted daughter hold a smouldering flame to a rocket's fuse, saw Kit check it was lit, saw him draw the child back. Up went the first rocket. Rose squealed.

"Missed," said Kit. "Look, the moon's still there."

"Next one!" Rose leaped up and down. "Next rocket, Kit! Quick, quick!"

The bonfire was a mound of flame. Brumous garden and marsh had disappeared into night. Wind spattered the sky with sparks. Rose ran to help her mother set the Catherine Wheel burning round and round. In the bucket of sand, burnt-out stumps tilted.

Alice fetched the pitchfork. As the pyre collapsed, she pushed branches into the centre. So practical she had grown . . .

Robert had been a practical man. Robert was still sailing out past Blakeney Point, *Whirlwind* reaching fast through the waves, slowly past the dunes because of the weight of the tide flowing inshore. Robert would always be sailing to sea as long as Alice was alive, gulls screeching round his mast.

He had left a good foreman at Durstead. Alice had worked hard at farming, she had learned a lot and she enjoyed it. It would be practical if she and Kit could make common cause . . . She silenced that thought, Kit would be hurt if he sensed her feeling that; if love wasn't a dream he wouldn't want it, would he, the fool.

Land to make pay, a child to bring up, practical . . .

Kit and Thérèse stood on the verge of the ruddy glare.

Alice wondered what they were talking about. Her, probably. They liked one another these days, those two; that was good, not that it would do any good.

He was so near, so near and so damned abstracted . . . As a boy he had seemed as liable to breakages as *Bittern*, nothing had changed. Old *Bittern* sold years back, probably broken up now . . . Guilt to overcome. Bad taste to acquit yourself altogether. Still didn't know if she had been guilty, but . . . The dead to outlive. Doing that. Ghosts to learn to live with. Practical . . .

Heat and smoke gusted her way. Alice stopped wondering what was the most seemly conduct of one's hauntedness, stepped back, wiped her eyes, leaned on her pitchfork. Life contrived to be peaceful and wretched at the same time – how was that? And why oh why wouldn't Kit come to share her peace? They'd never be happy if they didn't try, hearts are earned, blessedness is made by those who bless.

Rose dragged her mother away by the hand. She wanted to fetch potatoes to bake in the embers and ash.

III

Rose Clabburn carried her skates across the yard at Durstead. Past the wood-shed, icicles on the gutter, eiderdown of snow on the tiles. Past the game-larder where dead birds had their lolling heads gripped and then jerked down so there was a faint crunch and the sharp hooks jabbed through their lower jaws into their mouths and afterward little tufts of blood-stained feather remained on the hooks.

She knew it was silly to mind about how the pheasants and partridges were hung because it only happened after they were dead – but it was difficult to be sure the dead were not aware, she would prefer them not to be insulted. Silly too because she liked roast partridge, liked having recently learned to tell the difference between French and English partridges, liked the joke she had with her mother about could she tell the difference when they were plucked, gutted, roasted, and she was finding bits of shot in her mouth because, Alice said, not everyone shoots like your father shot. The great thing when trying hard not to imagine game-larder hooks in partridges' jaws was not to let your mind meander to the scullery instead and see again that rabbit being skinned.

The skates had been her Christmas present. She had slipped into the drawing-room time and again to contemplate the parcel under the tree, had tried to think her way through the wrapping. Then Christmas Day had come, the skates had been revealed, their steel glancing and pure, as inconceivable rusty as the silver trophies her father and her grandfather had won that stood on the dining-room sideboard.

Rose hugged her skates' soft red leather, raised them to her face, breathed their leather smell. On the evening of Christmas Day, then on Boxing Day evening, she had prayed for frost. Then every evening till New Year's Eve, then on to Twelfth Night. Mild days dawned, it rained sometimes. The rides through the woods stayed sodden and soft. The snowdrops under the lime trees by the tennis court came out. But now . . .

The snow creaked under her boots, she took a short-cut through the barn and the creaking stopped. One of the men was doing something to a tractor. There loomed the mountain range of straw bales where she was allowed to climb, the hay which smelled sweet and felt soft but she wasn't allowed to climb. Then out on the white field she could see the frozen pond, her heart thumped with joy, she ran.

Kit sat on the snow, wrestled his cold feet into pre-war leather cracked with age, supple with years of dubbin, that Robert must have been the last to put on. He wondered who would be the next man to wear these skates. He would be away across the Atlantic, some lover or husband of Alice would knot their hard old laces, no, more likely some lover or husband of Rose . . . Kit stood up, teetered forward. The rust-spotted blades wobbled on lengths of sedge frozen into the shallows, slid smoothly when the sedge was left behind.

Alice saw Kit coming, she wanted to dance, maybe she wasn't that practical after all, yes she was, but moments of delight could still visit her couldn't they, who would not give way to madness on a morning that white? She swept up to him, the long curved blades of her ancient fen-runners hissed through rime. Dance on ice now and to hell with forever. Dance now because your love may come to you now if ever, love only ever comes to the dancing and the mad, if it comes for a moment it's worth a lifetime, that's not saying much. And if your love doesn't come – at least you danced, there's gallantry in that, at least you waited, there's pride in that, at least you were defenceless.

She took his hand, shoulder to shoulder they skated round the irregular pond. Not as big as the broad at Fen House – hardly an acre. But a good enough ballroom for two, with the gabled barn in the background snow-thatched, Alice's horse and Rose's pony with their heads lowered to the hay chucked over the paddock fence. Left . . . Right . . . Long sweeping strides. Alice set the rhythm, she was the better skater, but Kit kept time, he lurched sometimes but he kept time. Left . . . Right . . .

The ice was white like a chalked ballroom floor. Alice flung her right hand up holding Kit's left hand, she spun in a pirouette. Nearly felled him – she should have said what she was going to do. Still, he recovered, on they whirled. This time she counted One, two, three, again she spun round. They laughed because they didn't fall; because the sky over the field was luminous pale blue; because Rose had gone down with a bump again and was sitting with her legs stuck out straight and her fair head and red hat cocked to one side.

Renounce, swished Kit's skates, Renounce, renounce. It is finer to give away than to clutch. Give away what you have loved most passionately, what is given away will not be befouled, what is kept is adulterated. The surrendered and the hoarded decay alike, but the surrendered doesn't stink.

Sometimes in the nervous restlessness of nightfall the invisible Alice of old came to him, he walked the London streets arm in arm with his abstract love – but she existed so faintly she soon vanished once more. He existed pretty tenuously himself for that matter; no doubt that was why it was easy to renounce what he was no longer able to desire very fiercely.

Ghostliness was a virtue – how else conduct one's mutability? It was honourable to vanish without complaint, the shadowy Alice of lost times taught Kit that. He must practise. He dropped her hand, skated away . . .

Back Kit swooped, they danced hand in hand, he was in time with Alice again, the powdery sshh sshh of their skates sounded together. Once more he left her. The white wood beckoned, this was a new beginning, his spirits lifted, he went further away, over by the dead reeds where Rose was tottering.

Back to where Alice was skating alone, her hands behind her back, blue neckerchief fluttering. Kit fell into stride with her, held out his hand. She smiled her slow smile straight into his eyes, her head flying past a background of snow field and snow trees, sparkling frosty air. She took his hand, he kissed her.

Rose's ankles ached. She had been swept staggering along by Alice, accidentally knocked down by Kit. She had developed a painstaking shuffle she could perform alone. She had taken her skates off, and then had much more fun skidding in her boots. Now she was tired.

Skates in her arms, she trudged back across the field. Clouds had come, she was shivering. This afternoon she might build a snowman, but now she would play with the puppies because the kitchen was warm.

The lurcher bitch lay in a basket with its walls falling down like a dilapidated stockade. Her bed was a couple of jerseys Rose had outgrown. She was suckling her litter, Rose hunkered down to watch, listening to the clock. Sometimes a puppy made a whimpering sound. One of them got pushed aside and seemed lost, Rose found it a teat to suck.

Then the kitchen grew lighter. She ran to the door, out into the yard. It was snowing again, soft white flakes swirling against the flint walls, the red brick sills, the gun-metal panes. Grey air sifted white, tracks began to be covered over.

Rose jumped and waved her arms.

"Snow!" she cried. "Snow, snow!"